T0355848

THANK YOU, GANDHI

ADVANCE PRAISE FOR THE BOOK

'This ingenious and moving book is a double search: a search for what it means to lead a Gandhian Life, and a searching examination of Gandhian Thought. Through the clever fictional meta device of reconstructing a friend's manuscript, Kumar provides a haunting portrait of modern India and discovers Gandhi has not disappeared. We cannot see him because we dare not look him in the eye'—Pratap Bhanu Mehta, former vice chancellor, Ashoka University

'A confluence of the personal, the political and the poetical, *Thank You, Gandhi* is a tribute to friendship and to the India that was and could be'—Namita Gokhale, writer and co-director of Jaipur Literature Festival

'A friendship becomes a metaphor for healing a nation, the act of writing itself a conversation between its past and present, and the Mahatma's experiments with truth serve as a tract for our time. *Thank You, Gandhi* is a remarkable book by one of our foremost educationists whose work, with courage and compassion, aims to reclaim our slipping common ground'—Raj Kamal Jha, chief editor, the *Indian Express* and author of *The Patient in Bed Number 12*

THANK YOU, GANDHI

KRISHNA KUMAR

PENGUIN
VIKING
An imprint of Penguin Random House

VIKING

Viking is an imprint of the Penguin Random House group of companies
whose addresses can be found at global.penguinrandomhouse.com

Published by Penguin Random House India Pvt. Ltd
4th Floor, Capital Tower 1, MG Road,
Gurugram 122 002, Haryana, India

First published in Viking by Penguin Random House India 2024

Copyright © Krishna Kumar 2024

All rights reserved

10 9 8 7 6 5 4 3 2 1

This is a work of fiction. Names, characters, places and incidents are either the
product of the author's imagination or are used fictitiously and any resemblance
to any actual person, living or dead, events or locales is entirely coincidental.

Please note that no part of this book may be used or reproduced in any manner
for the purpose of training artificial intelligence technologies or systems.

ISBN 9780670100002

Typeset in Adobe Caslon Pro by Manipal Technologies Limited, Manipal
Printed at Thomson Press India Ltd, New Delhi

This book is sold subject to the condition that it shall not, by way of trade
or otherwise, be lent, resold, hired out, or otherwise circulated without the
publisher's prior consent in any form of binding or cover other than that in
which it is published and without a similar condition including this condition
being imposed on the subsequent purchaser.

www.penguin.co.in

For Dr Charu Gupta and Dr Rushad Shroff

How could Gandhi be right when he was *odd*?

—Thomas Merton

The fire approached the great tree. The bird fanned the fire with its wings, hoping to put it out, but the tree burned away more fiercely. The bird sped to the spring, dipped its wings in the water, and rushed back to shake the water over the forest. The drops sizzled. It was not enough, not enough. The bird's entire body soaked in water was not enough to extinguish the fire.

—Thích Nhất Hạnh, The Ancient Tree

PART ONE

I

Munna is a nickname used throughout northern India to address boys. Its counterpart is Munni, used for small girls. Both have become so ubiquitous that now, few parents choose them as a specific nickname for their child. Earlier, this was not so. When my mother used it to address Viresh Pratap Singh some seventy years ago, his parents appreciated it so much that they switched over from the nickname Vir, which they had given him, to Munna. Vir suited his royal background more, but my mother's affection for him, and her own status as an educated woman in that small town in a princely state ensured that her choice prevailed. She had been appointed as the headmistress of the first-ever school for girls that Vir's uncle, the King, had established. At that time, central India had hardly any educated, let alone trained, women who could serve as teachers and headmistresses in schools for girls that the provincial government of the newly independent India was keen to promote. This region had not yet fully merged into the Union of India, so the King's initiative was highly appreciated. His brother, Viresh Pratap's father, rented out a part of his mansion to my parents who had come to this town as Partition refugees. They had lost the last of their belongings and had narrowly escaped with their lives before crossing over from Pakistan to the Indian side of Punjab. Despite this unimaginable calamity, they were able to strike fresh roots rather quickly in this faraway kingdom in central India because they were both highly qualified professionals. My father had been a practising lawyer in the High Court of Lahore. As for my mother, her graduate degree and teacher training qualifications were unique for a woman of an era where even the Queen was not all that literate. My mother's pioneer spirit and Punjabi energy to persuade local notables and others to hand over their daughters to her care in her school were appreciated by the royal clan. So, when my mother began calling V.P. Singh Munna, that nickname stuck.

Munna had vaguely curly hair, large light green eyes—quite typical of Bundela royalty—and a barely visible chin, amply compensated for by a prominent nose. By contrast, I had hardly any nose and outward-looking ears, like my father's. People must have wondered why I had failed to inherit my parent's long Punjabi nose. I suppose Munna's nose had to do for the both of us. Munna's mother was a delicate and beautiful, short-statured lady who held me in long hugs whenever she met me. Very few things kept her occupied in her mansion where servants lurked in every corner, one for every possible chore or errand. My mother, by contrast, was tall, hardy, and always busy running our newly established home without much help. At the same time, she managed all the various tasks and responsibilities that the first-ever school for girls in a conservative community involved. Amid all the commotion of her daily routine, my mother still found time to indulge Munna—and rather more time than she found for me, or so I thought.

Now the thing about Munna as a nickname is that, in most cases, it sticks for life. No matter how stout and masculine an adult a little Munna becomes, and no matter how high an office he occupies in his career, he continues to be called Munna in the family and by neighbours, early playmates and even perhaps by their offspring. This is how I too started calling VP, Munna, though he was a year older than me. We played the inconsequential games of early boyhood together with great vigour before cutting our teeth on cricket, hockey and badminton. Munna's father was, in fact, a member of the local cricket team and led it in some of the five-day-long test matches against the team of our neighbouring princely state.

Our boyhood days gave us generous opportunity for pranks, most of which were innocent though some were not. The main thing was that our parents, though markedly different in temperament and backgrounds, displayed a confident and jolly hands-off attitude towards the two of us and our bond of friendship, which was to last for life. It was only towards the end of our elementary grades that Munna's father declared his intention of sending him away to the Scindia School in Gwalior so that he might learn how to *ghitter-pitter* in English. Up until this point, we had both attended the new experimental school for a full eight years, some four miles away from the town in a forested location through which flowed a noisy and bubbling river.

Kundeshwar, as the place was called, was famous in the area for a Shiva temple built on a high sandstone promontory overlooking a tremendously deep pond formed, according to legend, by a meteor, millions of years ago. Our school was barely visible from the temple, surrounded as it was by tall mango, teak and neem trees. The school had been established by the interim provincial government of what was then known as Vindhya Pradesh, each of whose seven districts was a princely kingdom intent on setting its terms for agreeing to merge with the Union government of the newly independent nation. After Gandhi was assassinated at the end of January 1948, the minister in charge of education in the interim provincial government, who happened to be from our district and had participated in the Quit India Movement in the early 1940s, selected Kundeshwar as the site for an elementary school, where Gandhi's Nai Talim, or New Education, could be put into practice. There could have been no better location than the peaceful—yet rocky—sylvan Vindhya landscape.

Close to our school were the extensive orchards of mango and guava owned by Munna's uncle, the Maharaja. No one dared stop Munna and me from spending fine time among the orchards, climbing the trees and plucking raw fruit, or scaring away the parrots digging their strong red beaks into the ripening mangoes and guavas—depending on the season—before we could pick them. This was a paradise for two young boys before and after school, which itself was a grand experiment in child-centred education. The curriculum of our school was unique. The range of activities featured in it covered all the usual subjects but with more than a tinge of reinterpretation of the conventional knowledge these subjects stood for—and still do in several schools. We learned math from measuring cotton plants that we had ourselves sown and watered and weeded; watching them grow, caring for the buds as they developed. As for science, we learned it from the colours and oils used in creative ways—through skills such as book binding, dyeing thread, and spinning and weaving and cooking. And, of course, there was language—Hindi—that was enriched and enhanced by everything that we did with our own hands and discussed threadbare among ourselves and with our teachers. Even the Hindi grammar exercises prepared by our teachers were cyclostyled by us, children, on a Gestetner machine that we adored, cranking out sheet after sheet, one for each child . . . and perhaps a few more.

Along with a new Ambassador that he drove himself, Munna's father had an old green Dodge that chuntered with a brave racket along the not-so-smooth road flanked by mahua trees, four miles out of town to our school in Kundeshwar. The school day officially ended at 3 p.m.; Munna and I would engage in an intimate dialogue with the chatty driver, Bhagwandass, requesting him to let us take a swim in the river or climb the trees of mango or whichever fruit was in season, before heading back home. After such secret adventures and the school day's densely packed activities, we had plenty of time for long conversations in the backseat of the Dodge while going home. Neither of our fathers had any interest or idea about what our Gandhian school was imparting. They were satisfied that the school was being run well by the government. My mother also had little idea about what the Nai Talim associated with Mahatma Gandhi was all about, but she was greatly impressed with the little things that we brought home, which we had ourselves made at school. One day when Munna gave her a papier mâché cat that he had made and painted, she felt touched. When a few months later, he gave my father a sheet of handmade paper, he said, 'That's good', without taking a second look. But my mother was beside herself with joy and contentment—that a princely boy could do so much with his hands. She could spot in Munna a great seed of transformation—a seed that she thought would bring change to India.

Neither of our fathers had much truck or trade with Gandhi or for that matter, respect. In fact, as a Partition victim, my father harboured great resentment against Gandhi. Like millions of Punjabis displaced by the division of United India, he too believed that Gandhi should not have conceded to the British and Muslim decision to break up the old country. As for Munna's father, his cynicism, I realized much later, had to do with the popular view that Gandhi did not want India to industrialize and manufacture better cars than the Ambassador. He also did not agree with Gandhi's insistence that all education should be carried out in the child's mother tongue. When Munna finished grade 8 at the Kundeshwar school, his father thought it was high time that he learned English. Children of several royal families in Vindhya Pradesh had been educated at the famous Scindia School in Gwalior, and so Munna too was sent off there for his secondary schooling.

That left me bereft of the daily Dodge ride during my last year at the basic school. A year later, I was enrolled in the local high school. My friendship with Munna entered a new phase, adding fresh layers of dialogue and concerns as we progressed along our very different tracks, through institutional life, degrees and career. From Scindia, Munna went to the Daly College of Indore where many young scions of the central Indian princely states were sent to pick up the appropriate demeanour and conduct their fathers would require to be able to spot a suitable princely bride for them. Alas, Munna did not flourish at Daly, and soon enough he shifted to St Stephen's in Delhi. There he came into himself, focusing on what he wanted to do in life—serve in the Indian Administrative Service (IAS). Munna perceived the IAS as a means of living the ideals he had by now consciously cultivated. These ideals had to do with the dream of nation-building along Mahatma Gandhi's and Jawaharlal Nehru's vision of a modern yet kind, considerate nation which was also determined to alter its old self.

His father would have been happier if Munna would have chosen a career in the army. The status and pomp that military rank brought to the tiny feudal empires scattered throughout the rocky Vindhya mountains fascinated the royal fathers of male progeny. Munna's manifest tilt towards Gandhi's egalitarian ideas and arcane thoughts about progress had more than irked his father, so the choice of the IAS brought some relief, and admiration when entry into the haloed service was accomplished in the first attempt. The search for a suitable girl started right away, but it took time to spot a young woman educated sufficiently to perform her role as the district collector's wife. By the time Munna got his first posting in a not-too-distant district in the region, the Bundela clan's network in far-away Himalayan kingdoms, then a part of Punjab that would later become Himachal Pradesh, had thrown up a young, rather serious-minded elegant girl named Pushpalata. After marriage, her name became Pushpa. Her family did not particularly mind Munna's insistent refusal of dowry while cutting down on the clan's elaborate, hoary marriage ceremonies. Munna's father, however, didn't like all this and remained upset for some time. Rapid promotions ultimately landed Munna in the Bhopal Secretariat; it mollified Munna's father, who was actually apprehensive about what the young man might do next to shock his sensibilities. Poor soul, he didn't realize that his son was just as committed to non-violence as to Gandhi's vow of simplicity.

Munna and I had stayed in regular correspondence, exchanging weekly letters from the time he left for Scindia. I had known exactly how exasperated he felt at Daly before finding his feet and a sense of direction at St Stephen's, where he met a history teacher with profound insight into India's Gandhi-led struggle for freedom and the unwarranted outcome of Partition. In contrast to Munna's undergraduate experience in Delhi, my college and university education at a provincial institution had given me a somewhat cynical, but perhaps wider, earthy view of what India, Bhopal and Kashmir were going through after the two wars with Pakistan and a nationalist nuclear test. These wars and the famines that coincided with them had occurred during our college and university years in two very different institutional milieux. Bhopal and Kashmir had already experienced the tumult of Partition; during the wars with Pakistan, they suffered infrastructural damage that was going to remain invisible for a while.

As a civil servant, Munna had to work to make the 1975 Emergency a success, whereas I was free to criticize, it albeit not in public. We met twice during that period in Bhopal. On my second visit, he told me with some relief that he had got himself into the loop-line of helping the chief minister and the culture secretary work out the daily details of an art complex. This assignment had drawn Munna entirely out of the compulsion to deceive himself as a duty-bound admirer of Indira Gandhi's vision of a firmly controlled nation. She came to Bhopal to inaugurate the art complex. It was a great accomplishment and it ensconced Munna comfortably deeper among her young loyalists in the bureaucracy. This didn't work out well when she was assassinated less than a decade later.

The fires of unprecedented communal hatred that engulfed the Sikh men, women and children in many cities following Indira's assassination had barely subsided when a countless toll of the sick and the dead was caused in Bhopal by the poisonous gas that leaked from the Union Carbide pesticide plant. Munna was given the hard and personally risky job of looking after the hapless victims of the gas leak. At that time, I was teaching at a college in Delhi, staying not too far away from the Madhya Pradesh Bhavan where Munna, as a bureaucrat, was entitled to stay during his frequent visits. The graphic details of his work that he narrated during our evening conversations had plenty of signs, indicating that the administrative career he had chosen as his life's mission was now pulling his heart and mind apart. There was far too much to hide—and he had to do the hiding.

It was clear to me that Munna envied my freedom to feel cynical and distanced from the affairs of the State, teaching with passion and writing with freedom in a Hindi weekly. I seldom commented on the chicanery and diabolical choice of strategies politicians were routinely making; I didn't have to support or facilitate their work. Munna had to. India's new politics from now onwards consisted of unabashed vote-mobilization by playing with people's religious and caste identities. No region was now an exception. But the dark portents of the future were unmistakably rising from Ayodhya. Images and sounds to boost them had been telecast by State media for many years by now. The secular national elite was pleased that the Muslim novelist Rahi Masoom Raza wrote the script for the long Ramayana serial that showered tinsel on Ram and Sita's tragic story via satellite broadcast on a State-owned television channel on Sunday mornings. It was watched by women and men across the vast plains and plateaus of central and northern India. Munna was sure that the time was ripe for riots to begin and for Gandhi to shut up.

For a civil servant like him, exciting options were few. Radical political incursions in the social sphere meant that the fabric of religious and caste relations would become increasingly thin. After Advani had taken his Toyota-turned-chariot of Lord Rama for a junket across the subcontinent, the nation could only hold its breath. While it was so engaged, Rajiv Gandhi managed to douse Punjab's flames by using the former chief minister of our state as governor and top negotiator between rival factions. Rajiv, however, had muddied his boots elsewhere as well. Though he had engineered a sort of peace in Punjab and was no longer in power, he couldn't escape assassination at the hands of Sri Lankans.

A different India emerged from the army's attack on the Golden Temple, the Mandal riots, and the hysterical mobilization to demolish the Babri mosque in Ayodhya. The inauguration of a new, market-wedded economic policy suggested a curtain-raiser to a business-modelled nation, but the jubilation was interrupted in the winter of 1992 by wild hordes bringing down the Babri mosque before teatime. A phase in history ended that day. Peddlers of new hope were already at work, busy creating the Xanadu of what was to be known later as Digital India. It was a good time for my friendship with Munna to consolidate further as he was posted in various innocuous ministries in Delhi for nearly five years. He was by now a seasoned officer ready to serve whomever and whatever he could find in the IAS pecking order that was least painful for his bleeding soul. He knew that he wouldn't reach the heights reserved for the nimble and the deft in his fraternity, but that awareness did not bother him.

Both of us had lost our fathers by then, and my mother had moved in with me. She was a perennial fountain from which Munna drew much affection and solace he needed to keep his mind at peace, to remain calm and even creative. His princely training of touching the feet of the elderly and seeking their blessings, pleased my mother, as my upbringing had not given me that skill. That posture always irritated me. I sometimes made fun of Munna's habit, quoting Gandhi who had once reportedly said that only God's feet merited touching, suggesting that so much bending was not good for human dignity. Munna retorted that government service was all about bending and that for most, licking boots was a fine idea. At times, I wondered whether Munna felt he had chosen the wrong career, but he had never given me any real ground to confirm this impression. Within the haystack of government work, Munna had never failed to find enough needles to weave the threads of his Gandhian fantasies. Even as the arduous rehabilitation of the gas survivors in Bhopal stuttered, Munna had become involved in creating a museum of tribal lifestyles and art. His first posting as a novice IAS officer had been in a tribal district. While working on this museum project, Munna reconnected with his youthful ideas about the survival of tribal culture despite the brutal forces of development that were crushing all possibilities of benign co-existence from the Bastar forests in the east to the Narmada Valley in the west.

Munna perhaps had for a long time seen himself as a member of Gandhi's army, determined to save whatever could be saved; always ready to face my cynical barbs with good humour. When Nelson Mandela was released, a Swedish initiative in collaboration with the UN invited civil servants from many countries to visit sites of peaceful struggle. Munna was part of the Indian delegation that visited Robin Islands where Mandela had been imprisoned for twenty-six years. Munna brought a souvenir key of Mandela's cell for me and a tiny semi-precious stone vase that he purchased in a crafts market run by the government in Johannesburg. He was greatly impressed by what the South Africans had managed to do in record time to promote heritage crafts. During this same stay, Munna also visited the places associated with Gandhi in Transvaal and Natal, ruminating all the time on what he might push through Delhi's craft technocracy, whose laser-like vision could only focus on tourism and export markets. Over the following years, Munna pursued an assignment on the side to commemorate Kamaladevi Chattopadhyay by proposing a centre for education and training in culture resources. As it always seemed to happen, he had to do the bricks-and-mortar job of seeing through the land acquisition in far-off West Delhi and the construction of a modest campus. By the time the institution was ready to start functioning, Munna had been recalled to Bhopal.

When we had met after a few weeks, during his visit to Delhi, he had told me that Bhopal had lost track. He was distressed by the fact that Bhopal's cultural activities had now become the privilege of a narrow, self-serving elite. One characteristic of such an elite is its blissful isolation from all that goes on around them. The Bhopal elite enjoyed their life and status while the ethos of the city went through a metamorphosis—from being an example of secular vernacularity to becoming a post-Gujarat symbol of the political ambitions of the Hindu Right. Bhopal had also now emerged as a commercial learning hub; educational institutions settled here to play second fiddle to the burgeoning coaching industry.

What happened in the summer of 2019 was, therefore, not altogether unexpected. The results of the parliamentary elections held over April/May 2019 finally started coming in on 23 May. It was the height of summer and the temperature in Delhi was already approaching 45 degrees Celsius by late morning when NDTV discussants of trends had settled into their expert roles, ready with interpretations. Counting in the Bhopal constituency was showing an early marked trend in favour of the Hindu nationalist candidate, but the result was still awaited late that night when I went to sleep. My landline rang before sunrise. It was Munna. His voice sounded thin and distracted. All he said was 'K., we couldn't save Bhopal.' I found myself saying that it should bring no surprise to him, but before I could finish the sentence, I realized that Munna had put the phone down. Such a thing had never happened before. He must be shattered, I thought, and it wasn't hard to guess why. The city of Bhopal, that he had served in so many different capacities, was now going to be represented in the nation's Parliament by someone who had publicly described Mahatma Gandhi's assassin as a great patriot. Like many candidates, the one in Bhopal was under judicial scrutiny for several grim charges. One might say that these were just charges, and they might prove false in the end. Publicly avowed appreciation of Nathuram Godse, the killer of Gandhi, was a different matter.

It was not just an opinion or a passing fad; it was embedded in a well-wrought ideology. By fielding that particular candidate from Bhopal, the clever strategists of the ruling party had in a way announced the obliteration of the old, cultured world of Bhopal. The historical part of the city had already faced death in the tens of thousands of men, women and children who had collapsed after inhaling methyl isocyanate more than three decades earlier. Now, a more permanent inferno was to be the city's destiny, with no prospect of a purgatory.

I thought Munna must have felt utterly lost and lonely at that moment, in his Noida home. I took out my car and drove out of Delhi and across the long Nizamuddin bridge over the heat-hit, virtually dry Jamuna to be with him. The bridge was virtually empty during the early hours. The air was still quite smoky, yesterday's evening dust still hanging. The rising sun's light made the journey tedious, except for the strong urge in me to be with Munna, no matter how early it was. The guard at the gate of the Deluxe apartment complex in Sector 56 was familiar with my number plate. I parked close to Munna's first-floor flat, stepped out of the car and climbed upstairs. The bell below the name Viresh Pratap Singh didn't take more than a short press before Pushpa opened the screen door. As I stepped in, she directed me to the room where Munna had put together a considerable collection of books, mostly acquired since his retirement. The room had two upholstered easy chairs, both transported from Munna's princely home long ago. They were the kind of chairs that used to occupy the four corners of the big royal drawing room. At the centre of this room were sofa sets arranged around a central table that had carved legs. It stood on a white spotted deerskin rug, covering a Persian carpet extending out to the seating. Munna was sitting motionless in one of those chairs.

I tapped him on the shoulder to announce my presence before sitting opposite him. He smiled, so did I, but it was obvious how we felt. I had to initiate and sustain our conversation that morning, desperately trying to convey that what had occurred had been in the offing for an awfully long time and that no one knew it better than he. We recalled a conversation we had had in 1981 when the symbol of a lotus flower was blithely granted to the present-day ruling party. The only one who had objected, citing the obvious association of the lotus with Hindu symbolism and rituals, had been Arjun Singh who was at that time the chief minister of Madhya Pradesh, and Munna, along with his senior officer, reported directly to Singh about the progress of the cultural complex designed by Charles Correa. Singh passed away in 2012, but my reference to that lotus episode somewhat cheered Munna up, reviving in him older resonances of India's deceptive selfhood. Somewhat perking up, he asked, 'Why just the lotus in 1981? Wasn't the symbol of *deepak* granted to the Jan Sangh under Nehru?' He was right of course. Deepak, as a symbol, was more embedded in Hindu rituals than the lotus. After all, a little earthen lamp is more ubiquitous than the lotus flower which doesn't blossom in every pond in our vast land. We laughed at this shared observation. So, we agreed that what had hit Bhopal now was hardly a meteor from Mars where, incidentally, India had tried to land its smart little space rover quite recently. The rover, sadly, didn't prove to be as obedient as India's people. The morning ended with Pushpa offering us breakfast. I hadn't told my wife, still asleep, where I was going so I called home. As we ate, I noticed from his expression that Munna was back to brooding.

Later that week, Pushpa phoned to tell me that her husband had not been feeling well. They were friends with the owner of a nearby private nursing home. The doctor there examined Munna, finding nothing particularly wrong. His blood test also showed the usual figures, indicating mildly high levels of sugar.

Munna decided that it might be a good idea to be examined thoroughly at AIIMS, where retired IAS officers had permanent provisions for such requirements. When he reported how he felt, the doctor, who had known him for a long time, decided to do an MRI. The results indicated that Munna had suffered an 'inconsequential stroke'. There was nothing to worry about said the doctor: such small things usually sort themselves out with good care and exercise. I wasn't fully convinced, so I called up our common friend, Ravi, who like us was from MP. Ravi had studied neurology overseas. I told him what I knew about Munna's ill health vaguely and asked him if something needed to be done.

Ravi was not the kind of doctor who would offer advice over the phone. He said he would like to see Munna, and so, he and I drove off to Noida. Munna was a bit surprised when we showed up at his door. He quickly realized that he would have to submit to Ravi's reflex tests—which included having his knee joint tapped with a little brass hammer, and the toes and soles of his feet brushed across with a sharp pin. And it didn't end there. There was no stopping Ravi once he became intrigued by some aspect of a case he had noticed. He now began a long and pointed conversational probe to gauge every detail of Munna's moods over the past weeks. Initially, Munna was quite reluctant to speak about the effects of the election results. I'm sure he thought that it would look foolish if he mentioned the outcome in Bhopal as something worth brooding about. But all three of us were so familiar with the world of Bhopal that after a few apparently casual and rambling questions, Ravi was able to trace the source of Munna's condition, which he termed an 'emotional event'.

One thing about Ravi is that you can count on his remaining jolly and buoyant. He cheered us both up by joking about the winner in Bhopal. 'If it's someone involved in terror stuff, Gandhiji

will look after the matter,' said Ravi. 'Didn't he browbeat so many
patriotic terrorists in his time?' When we finished chuckling,
Ravi said that he agreed with his AIIMS colleague's diagnosis
and line of treatment, but he wanted to add some medication. In
those days, Ravi had been experimenting with mixed therapies,
featuring ayurvedic herbs. Munna was interested in such things.
Over the next fortnight or so, he gobbled some colourful
ayurvedic capsules to nourish and rejuvenate the mind's deeper
energies. The next thing I heard from him was that he was
planning to write a book, and before setting out on the project,
he would spend a month in Mumbai with his daughter and a
second month with his sister living in Kentucky.

These were excellent plans I thought, to restore my old
friend's health and spirit, which had sustained him through
a career studded with the implementation of wicked policies.
The worst of these had come in the last patch of his career. The
promotion of the Aadhaar card—imparting a unique identity
to every citizen—had stoked Munna's deepest resentment.
He had no choice but to push the implementation of the
Aadhaar scheme. At that point, I was serving an apex national
organization concerned with education. In this position, I had
hoped to create space for critical thinking in different subjects.
Apart from handling endless controversies plaguing textbook
change, I was learning to take the Right to Information (RTI)
in my stride. Its promulgation into law was widely perceived
as the nation's best fast-forward for democratic transparency.
While RTI was enabling every covert Tom, Dick and Harry
within the organization to undermine it by demanding every
possible file note, the beautiful Aadhaar was allowing the State
machinery to gently coax every citizen to share their bio-socio-
physical information in the name of efficiency. Munna had
predicted that soon enough all citizens would become naked
and the State fully opaque.

It would reverse all the steps taken towards decentralization of power and authority, Munna used to say. It would pave the way for the birth of a digitally competent surveillance State, eventually squeezing the last drop of blood out of the hard-won rights to privacy and personal freedoms. These dire predictions were destined to come true later, under a regime determined to control and remodel the country.

Munna wrote a few times from his daughter's home in Mumbai and later on from his sister's in Kentucky. He seemed to be in a buoyant mood, working away on a book about which he divulged no details whatsoever. I assumed it must be an autobiographical account of his administrative career. Decades ago, he had asked me to read a book titled *Told by an Idiot* in order to get a grip on what it meant to be an administrative officer in central India. The book was the autobiography of R.C.V.P. Noronha, who had served our region under British rule as a member of the haloed Indian Civil Service (ICS). When the central region was reunified in 1956 under a new state called Madhya Pradesh, Noronha was appointed as its first chief secretary. His autobiography has a mixture of inspiring stories and cynical commentary, which is probably why Munna recommended the book.

More recently, Munna had urged me to read Arjun Singh's autobiography, published after his death in 2012. We found many enlightening details in Singh's account of the Bhopal disaster— it happened during his leadership of Madhya Pradesh—and his subsequent role in calming the inferno of Punjab. Munna did not agree with everything that Arjun Singh had said about the gas tragedy. He felt that no single narrative could ever suffice to describe the hydraheads of the catastrophe. I was sure Munna's own account would offer some uneasy revelations, so I was glad to imagine that the writing project occupied him fully, instead of carrying on hopelessly about the 2019 election outcome in Bhopal.

That was not the case. The visits with his daughter and his sister had undoubtedly given him a break, but as soon as he returned to Delhi, his persistent feeling that everything was going wrong and that a certain wickedness had overcome politics, returned. During his absence, Kashmir had been re-carved brutally. It wasn't just the suddenness with which the decision to reorganize Kashmir and immobilize all its senior leaders had been revealed; what was particularly sad was that the Opposition was caught napping. Some among them openly supported the abrogation of Article 370, thereby helping the ruling party to feel that what it was doing was not just clever, but also legitimate. Munna was also dejected by the furtive shelving of habeas corpus petitions from Kashmir at the highest level of the judiciary. To his perception that 'they will destroy everything', the high-speed clearance to the Citizenship Amendment Act (CAA) proved to be another blow. In those days, Munna frequently visited me and when he didn't visit, he would make long phone calls, distress and despair resonating in his voice.

Earlier that summer, we had visited our senior friend and inspiration, the space scientist Yash Pal at his Noida flat. It was obvious that his wonderful life was nearly over. Curled up on his sofa, unable to move unassisted, Yash Pal removed his signature pipe—unlit—from his lips, and asked us, 'Should we give up on India?' Munna was quick to answer, 'Not yet.' Now, only a few months later, I suspected that he had done just that in the secret chambers of his mind. The CAA, which was so blatantly discriminatory against Islam, was being hailed as a masterstroke. The courts seemed ready to swallow it, just as they had been ready to swallow the unstated erasure of *habeas corpus*. Why inconvenience the government, the judges seemed to say in verdict after verdict. The judge who had proved most convenient of all had been nominated for the Rajya Sabha soon after his retirement.

Then came Shaheen Bagh, rekindling the old hope that the culture of protest nurtured by Gandhi was not fully dead. A senior woman journalist believed that the fact that Muslim women had gathered in such large numbers for a sustained sit-in at Shaheen Bagh could prove to be the turning point. Within a few days of the start of this unprecedented demonstration, many public figures, academics and writers—not just media persons—began to visit the site. Nevertheless, I was somewhat surprised when I got a call from Munna to say that he too had been there, asking me if I would come along with him one day. I generally keep aloof from activism and in fact, I don't like that word—it suggests that being active can be a profession. However, I could not say 'no' to Munna. I thought he might have found it somewhat awkward to be recognized in that crowd as a retired civil servant, so, he wanted me as a companion. We fixed a date in the following week and met a short distance away from Shaheen Bagh.

As Munna emerged from his grey Hyundai, his light blue T-shirt flagged a sudden return to youth and hope in someone, who, a few months earlier, had felt so debilitated. As we walked past several police barriers and came closer to the site, we noticed how stereotypically Muslim the ethos was, created by the women's dress and babies sitting on their laps. They were not activists. They were ordinary. Nor did they seem pushed from behind by a political faction using them as a cover. Munna said they reminded him of Bhopal. The huddling together, the lack of prosperity in the community and a sense of bewilderment were obvious. Or maybe he was reading too much into the unusual sight, pouring into it his anger with the government and his ebbing desire to see resistance to the unabashed jolt the India he had served was receiving. He had devoted his career and personal energy to making India survive the venality and callousness of political leaders he was obliged to

work for. For me too, Munna's India was real, but my cynicism
had saved me from the shock he had received. The evening at
Shaheen Bagh elated him, but the hustle of so many disparate
and jarring elements around, and not just the police, made us
uneasy as we departed. Things could suddenly go wrong under
a dispensation that doesn't appreciate protests—any protest.

Before anyone could guess how exactly things would go
wrong, they did. Shaheen Bagh became a symbol and spread to
several cities. The false hope that the spirit of India had found
the right and narrow crack through which its rays could slip
free had grown like a bonsai when its master was inattentive.
The denouement came just as unpredictably as had the Muslim
women's inexplicable determination to come out of their
homes and demonstrate in the open. That's not how Muslim
womanhood is imagined, remembered or even caricatured.
No chapter of India's modern minoritism history holds such
an episode among its layered memory. Perhaps the Turkish
women had done it; perhaps the Uzbek women had done it.
Poor Muslim women of India had never sat together like this,
for every believer in the Constitution to notice and admire. The
last time I had seen Muslim women together, forming a little
colourful crowd, was in the opening scene of the film *Bombay*.
The scene carried A.R. Rahman's melodious song, 'Kehna hi
kya', which figuratively translates as, 'It's so wonderful'. Shaheen
Bagh was just like that: the dream of awakened India fulfilled
without education or even literacy, without equality, without
much politics.

The fantasy was smashed by the bull called Donald Trump,
the Republic Day guest. By the time he reached Delhi after
first stopping in Gujarat, riots had broken out in the eastern
periphery of the Capital. The news bulletins suddenly became
more familiar: people killing and getting killed in the dark hours,
and in the shining hours too; the police stood by watching,

waiting for the word that there was sufficient smoke, bodies
and wounds for them to restore law and order. College teachers,
students, writers and lawyers had adequately got entangled in
the web of WhatsApp for cases to begin against them. Trump's
wife Melania was attending a special class of the Happiness
Curriculum in a school in South Delhi as homes, shops and
a school burned in East Delhi. And in the middle of all of
this, the coronavirus arrived. Shaheen Bagh was now buried
as a pleasant pre-corona memory. Delhi and the rest of India
were in for the new, long phase of denotified normalcy. Neither
Munna nor I took the new virus seriously for several weeks. We
were like the World Health Organization whose Cypriot chief
hesitated for quite some time to say that something unusual
was around.

The riots left Delhi somewhat dazed, as had the riots that
had broken out after the assassination of Indira Gandhi, thirty-
six winters ago. Now too it felt as if citizens knew in their hearts
what had happened, but nobody was talking. In hospitals and
schools of East Delhi—the epicentre of violence—doctors and
teachers resumed their daily chores without a word. Schools
stayed shut for a few days, but hospitals looked after the
wounded throughout the riots. There was no point asking why
so many were suddenly showing up with wounds and burns.
When classes were resumed, teachers taught the syllabus from
the pre-riots point onwards. No one wondered why only a
handful of children had returned.

Arrests were being made daily; many of these were made
under laws that denied bail. Quite a few well-known names,
some of whom we knew personally, were charged for instigating
the riots. Munna was feeling disgusted and angry. On my part,
I felt better prepared. Half a century ago, when I was a student,
my father had dissuaded me from considering his profession,
law, as my career. After his death, I had from time to time

looked at his book on police diaries. It was all about how a vigilant lawyer should read police records and sort out the mix of high cleverness and incompetence—not to mention orders from political masters—characteristic of police's first-level documentation of a crime. A few pages of my father's book are enough to make you realize that all hope of reform in the gargantuan police system, which the British had assembled to replace practices extant since Mughal times—without entirely abandoning or suppressing them—had been in vain. Now, the Delhi Police were dealing with digital stuff, weaving a grand story of a conspiracy intended to malign the nation during the visit of the world's most powerful leader, who was to be the chief guest of our post-colonial republic's most sacred day.

Although Munna was deeply unhappy about the manipulative dispersal of Shaheen Bagh, he told me that he was not going to worry about the police story. Instead, he was now going to focus on his book. As for me, I attempted to contact a senior police officer, the husband of one of my former students. I wanted to get some inkling of the reality, but he never picked up the phone, and I decided not to pursue this with his wife. Munna felt that I was being unnecessarily bothered. How could somebody under orders to compose a narrative tell you the facts, he asked. Perhaps he was right and actually, there were no worthwhile facts, and the only reality was murky. Delhi's air carried it with superb calm and composure. The daily counts of what they call 'particulate matter' of various sizes were soaring. The new virus might be the latest 'particularity'.

When the lockdown was suddenly announced, a week was left in the month of March. New social norms to contain the epidemic were already in place. These norms had helped throw out the last Muslim women clinging in a tiny symbolic huddle at Shaheen Bagh. The provisions of the lockdown were quite bewildering; how the vast population of marginal workers in large cities would cope with daily needs took no time to surface as a big puzzle. It was like a repeat of demonetization —dramatic and clueless about its consequences. Tens of thousands of daily wagers and labourers marched to the bus terminus named after the tenacious medieval Rajput hero, Maharana Pratap, desperately hoping to find a means of transport to exit Delhi. Thousands of others were stranded in the vast slums of East Delhi, with no income to pay the rent or purchase food. In response to this deepening crisis, the local authorities mobilized non-governmental organizations to arrange food daily in some of the poorest colonies of riot-hit North-East Delhi and adjoining areas.

I wasn't surprised when I heard from Munna that he had decided to join an NGO which was distributing two meals a day to migrant workers in a colony not far from Noida. On hearing this, my first thought was about the fast-spreading coronavirus, being reported every morning and evening by the media. I conveyed my concern, but Munna said he was taking adequate precautions. His voice on the telephone lost its usual pitch for a moment when he told me that the people he was feeding were construction labourers from our district in Madhya Pradesh. It made instant sense that Munna had found a source of coherence in the middle of administrative chaos and emotional misery. His habitual yearning for self-sacrifice had found yet another means of satisfaction. The price of this sacrifice took less than a fortnight to reveal itself.

Soon enough, the case counts were growing by the hour across the National Capital Region, as in the rest of India. Anxious as I felt, there was nothing I could do apart from calling up my friend every few days. My apprehension for his safety increased, but he seemed to have mentally returned to his days as a dedicated IAS officer, determined to help the poor and the dying in gas-struck Bhopal. Dissuading him from exposing himself to the virus by carrying on as an official volunteer for the distribution of food might have been possible had I personally gone to his house, but that could not happen due to the lockdown.

It was a hot evening in the third week of April when I saw this email in my inbox:

Dearest K.,

They did a corona test on me as I wasn't feeling too well and declared me positive. I don't quite know what that means but you know it can mean anything. I don't want to alarm you, but I'm attaching eight files with this mail. I thought I must pass them on to you just in case the worst transpires. These files contain what I have been trying to write all these months. You know I'm not a writer like you and you may find that the stuff is nothing but emotional drivel, unsuitable for publication in our changed world. But I thought you might find here and there something worth looking at for our joint satisfaction, and it will be great if you find it worth re-organizing and refining for a wider audience. That would be wonderful indeed, and let's hope we both can enjoy seeing this work out in public. In any case, let me hope for the best for now, relieved as I feel, consigning these files to your safe custody.

Greatest love and best wishes.

Pushpa called two days later saying that things had taken a turn for the worse. Munna needed to be taken to the private nursing home in the neighbourhood that he was familiar with, but they had none of the facilities needed to look after a corona patient. He was shifted to AIIMS, where things seemed promising. Ravi and I visited the institute but weren't allowed to go near the ward where Munna was isolated. A resident doctor told us that Munna's high blood pressure and somewhat high sugar levels were posing a problem, but he was struggling rather well for now, so there was hope. It stayed like that for ten days when the news came that he had started to sink. It was terrible to realize that nobody might be able to come from his home, although his daughter, who had already acquired the necessary permission to drive from Mumbai, had started off in her car. She had also alerted the son of the old family priest who had served the royals for nearly half a century. As small boys, we used to wait for the sugar-coated peanuts that he would offer us after completing the evening prayer at a large temple near the fort, not far from Munna's home. Sometimes he would let us beat the drum during the service. After the priest's death, his son had assumed the temple duties handed down in the Bundela royal establishment for centuries. Hearing that Munna's life was feared for, the young priest immediately obtained permission from the district officials to travel to Delhi. He arrived barely hours before Munna passed away.

We were merely four grieving souls, so the stringent corona funereal controls didn't affect us as we stood around the unlit pyre at the desolate Noida crematorium. The late afternoon air was hot and dusty. The priest was reluctant to allow Munna's daughter to light the flames and instead turned to me. The All India Institute's official was standing by in his PPE—Personal Protective Equipment—giving an outer-space feel to the empty crematorium. The priest chanted aloud the various holy verses that included a few particular to the Bundela princely clans to which Munna belonged while guiding me to perform the last rites.

II

A sense of pointlessness, accompanied by physical exhaustion penetrated every aspect of my life that week. It had all happened so suddenly, imparting a ghastly reality to the coronavirus which had so far gone unseen and felt inconsequential. The collective banging of *thalis* and lighting of *diyas*, as suggested by the nation's leader, had given a certain festive feel to the contagion. Patriotism and disease seemed to be having a nice contest. But now, with Munna gone, it was hard to escape a rounded realization that everything had gone wrong.

The old priest had insisted on taking the ashes to Allahabad. He then wanted to go to Ayodhya to perform a special ritual at the temple built more than a century ago by the Bundela clan. There was no way of dissuading this priest, so official permission letters were procured to enable him to travel during lockdown. A taxi was arranged so he could reach the destination and do the spiritual needful. I'm not sure if Munna would have approved of or bothered with all this for someone else. He had lived his careful life walking a narrow path that he had paved himself—between his princely background and his cherished personal ideals. After his sudden disappearance, scenes of our childhood and school days shone through the grief of his death and the general gloom of politics and disease that was around the city of Delhi and the nation. His last email had perhaps conveyed a premonition which I had not recognized, or maybe that too is simply a way of talking about such a thing.

During the summer of 2019, when the outcome in Bhopal struck him hard after the parliamentary elections, I should have realized that Munna was struggling with inner turmoil. Perhaps he wanted to cut himself off from the radical new reality of India. But he was much too idealistic and energetic to reveal such a secret wish. One couldn't judge his state of mind when he left for America to visit his sister. On his return, he seemed hopeful—of a break in the political trajectory sooner than anyone else might have thought. That is how he interpreted Shaheen Bagh, an unexpected protest site—as a turning point.

Between that break and the terrible violence of Hindu–Muslim riots that coincided with Donald Trump's visit in February 2020, there was no room to entertain illusions of a recovery. The spread of coronavirus looked as if nature had supplied its response to the perfidy pursued by humans. But then, one had to recognize the global character of the virus; one had to be scientific about it. Munna must have caught the virus while letting his desire to help the poor override his scientific awareness. The scenes being shown on television, of poor migrant labourers walking hundreds of kilometres, would have further saddened my friend. At times, I felt that he had chosen his moment of withdrawal rather sensibly. I read his last email several times, but I didn't feel like opening those attachments for nearly a month. I must say I was not curious as I had convinced myself months earlier that Munna was writing autobiographical accounts like many IAS officers do when they feel somewhat free from the constraints of service rules thanks to retirement.

But apart from a lack of curiosity, there was reluctance too. Munna's email had clearly assigned me a posthumous duty. I wasn't sure that I could fulfil it, or rather, that I would be able to exert myself to be able to properly fulfil Munna's last worldly wish. For the previous two years, I had been struggling with a book of my own which aimed at providing an autobiographical account of a rare administrative experience that I had as the head of a national level institution. This book had been dragging on for a decade since the end of my term in that organization. The effort to delve into the details of the political ethos in which I had achieved success had mutated during this decade, becoming an emotional dilemma about what was worth revealing to the world in a hostile environment. This dilemma had pushed my book deeper and deeper into the search for the perfect narration suited to the fragile atmosphere surrounding all writing and acts of expression. I could not abandon the effort in order to turn towards other, more doable professional projects that I had set up for myself since retirement. Facing these difficulties of my own, I could hardly avoid feeling burdened with an unusual responsibility when I read Munna's last message that he wanted me to bring his project to completion.

Not knowing what exactly that project was helped me for a few weeks, but one afternoon towards the end of May, I opened two of the eight attachments he had sent. The instant effect was confusion, excitement and anxiety. The confusion arose from the common title of all the attachments, the excitement from the surprise this common title created, and the anxiety from the instant doubt of whether what Munna had apparently tried to do was capable of being accomplished in the times from which he had fortuitously exited.

All eight files had a similar name and were distinguished only by the number following the name. The first file was named 'G1', the second 'G2' and so on. I opened 'G1' and started reading the first page, but I gained no specific clue as to what the 'G' might stand for. I glanced at the next couple of pages with no better result, so I decided to get back to reading slowly rather than scanning to satisfy my curiosity. Munna had talked about an old, dried-up well into which he wanted to look deeply enough to see across the dry grass and darkness beyond which he apparently expected some water waiting to be touched. The metaphor was so arduously pursued for nearly twenty lines that I could not avoid the impression that he was preparing to talk about his childhood. At that time, our little princely town had large, strongly built wells at all four corners and three in the centre. These were so well built that one might say they were designed to serve as social sites. They buzzed with sounds of people talking right from early morning through the long afternoons to the evenings and into the night. People who came to the wells kept changing throughout the day according to some neat plan. Early mornings were reserved for women. Before dawn, they came for a bath and later to fetch water in shining brass vessels, which they carried home stacked on their heads.

As the morning got brighter and turned into forenoon, one saw men, young and old, using the platforms around the wells to wash their clothes before taking a leisurely bath finished off by a full bucket tipped over the head. The sound of the pulleys taking the buckets down and up the wells filled the air all day long. Another group of women arrived towards the evening and later on, a few men stopped by to get some water they would use as part of their worship at the nearby temples.

Deeply etched as they were in the memory of my childhood, these routines quickly resurfaced in my mind because of the

long opening paragraph of the first attachment which ended
with the elaborate digging done all over the town to lay piped-
water lines. This had occurred nearly a decade after the merger
of our princely state into the Indian republic, in 1948 or 1949.
Munna's description of this great transition, leading to the end
of a well-centric culture, created a strong impression that the
book he had been working on was indeed an autobiography.
That's what I had suspected all along. Now that my suspicion
was beginning to find a vague confirmation, I felt anxiety rising
in me about how difficult it might be to persuade a reasonable
publisher to take up a piece of writing left behind by an IAS
officer who hadn't published a word in his life and was therefore
quite unknown.

The next few pages showed how erroneous—and
misplaced—my initial thoughts and the worry, which they
had provoked, were. Munna's prose became contemplative as
its subject veered closer and closer to what is popularly known
as 'development'. This glorified term was strongly associated
in government parlance with villages during our boyhood.
The tight fit between development and villages was encoded
in the unquestionable goal of 'rural development' to which
every administrator, provincial or national, young or old,
was supposed to be committed as inseparably as he might be
assumed to be dedicated to the Republic itself. Munna's prose
created this web of ideas and in the centre of it, I felt, I saw the
meaning of 'G.'

'G' had to be for 'Government', I told myself, and so the
book was, after all, going to be autobiographical. Surely some
publisher would find it useful as a text to push into the libraries
of institutions of public policy and management, in addition
to those dedicated to coaching aspirants for competitive exams
of central and state civil services. Most such outfits were
private and preferred buying precisely the kind of books that

offer knowledge about governance issues accumulated through inspiring experience and are laced with the new national imagination that the liberalized economy called upon aspirants to cultivate.

As I cast a glance at the bottom of the computer screen, I saw that this file contained more than seven thousand words. If Munna's book was about what I thought it was at this stage of my investigations, then I didn't need to go any further in the script that this file contained. It would be better, I thought, to peep at the next file, 'G2', and make sure that the book really was about Munna's administrative life and wisdom. The very first line of 'G2' showed how wrong I was.

It was about the beating of a woman, a scene from Munna's childhood that he had shared with me during one of our rides to the basic school in his car. That memory of our conversation had faded to such an extent in my mind that the opening paragraph of 'G2' came across like a horrible video—the kind which the BBC might warn its viewers about, saying it contains disturbing images. The whole narrative was disturbing from beginning to end with screams and blood and a hockey stick. The woman was a maidservant who fetched water for Munna's and my family. I recalled her face, and the two big shining brass vessels balanced on her head, but what was she doing here in this book? My eyes skimmed across the text as if running home to escape from something we dare not understand. But there was no escape here, as one description of horror followed another with words serving as silent knives slicing the slumbering consciousness of a violent world.

I soon came upon a paragraph describing the thrashing of three boys in my high school. I had told Munna about this incident when he was visiting from Scindia for summer holidays. Finding that incident narrated here in graphic freshness, with an interpretive sentence that I didn't at all remember having spoken as it was not a part of my awareness at the time, my confusion and sense of puzzlement rose and rose as I read on and on. Stories of violence and human brutality derived from intimate knowledge led to bigger, public stories like those of Hitler's concentration camps.

I scrolled down the long text, wondering how these descriptions of violence might connect with the text I had read in parts in the first file. Was it all a rambling, unshaped noting of ideas by a disturbed mind? Perhaps I would have to look at the other files to figure out the theme that Munna was pursuing. Surely, he wouldn't have sent me these files as a parting gesture had they not contained something that was of great importance to him. To expect that I would be able to complete his project seemed somewhat irrational, if not purely emotional. That he entertained such a thought indicated how much he trusted me, a long-time friend, and also his confidence in the importance of what he was trying to put across in writing in what were the last few months of his life.

Scrolling down further, picking out a sentence here, a phrase there, I came across a paragraph about lynching. This was surely not either a personal experience of childhood or later life. Wide-eyed and a bit nervous from having to deal with a shapeless act of expression, I read a full paragraph in which a contemporary news story of a Muslim boy being lynched and killed on a train approaching Delhi was narrated. The story was followed by an unhesitating analysis of current politics. Over the recent years, lynching incidents have been accepted as routine by the political leadership while the press and television maintain a voluntary or perhaps secretly enforced hesitancy to give any real significance to such incidents. They were occurring so frequently and the desire to cover them with any sense of earnestness was receding in the public media so seemingly naturally, that one couldn't even say that Indian society was changing or that its fabric was coming apart. If Munna's files were a portrait of *this* change, it would be impossible to find a reasonable publisher no matter how hard I worked on the text to make it acceptable.

I began to feel sorry for myself that thoughts of such banal practicality had assailed my mind when I ought to be feeling sentimental at being in possession of an honest piece of writing by a life-long friend whom I had suddenly lost. But the more I glanced at the text facing me, the more uncomfortable and embarrassed I felt. A long and complicated sentence ushered me into an association that I could hardly appreciate at that moment. Perhaps it was because I had been looking at the screen for a long time and felt somewhat fatigued. It was late on a hot afternoon in May, with the street outside my house completely silent because of the lockdown. A pair of lapwings disturbed the silence every few minutes with their loud and shrill instructive voices, saying, 'Did he do it? Pity to do it?' But to me, they seemed to be saying, 'Don't do it! Don't do it!'

I felt I must close the screen when an impossibly complex sentence conveyed Munna's simple thesis that the centre of Indian culture had moved to enable a new culture of governance to take over. It sounded like someone talking aloud using big words not quite worked out in necessary detail, just like the lapwing flying around outside. The sentence went on to claim that personal convenience was where India's old, generous civilization had found its new core, to match the government's new discovery that administration would become quite cool if people's diverse urges and aspirations could be directed against Muslims and other religious minorities.

This model, Munna suggested, had been adopted after its proven success in 2002 in Gujarat and the government had continued replicating it through new laws that made any voicing of concern over circumstances a risky affair. A few cases were sufficient to communicate the potentially sensitive voices that were left unmodified—that if they became any louder, there would be little chance of remedial legal action or effective protest by sympathizers even if they could form a little crowd on the winding street called Jantar Mantar at the edge of Connaught Place. Manage your emotions and continue your daily life with the conveniences you are used to—remember that you were not born to be a hero, the government seemed to say. India had moved on, Munna's text indicated at the end of the paragraph I was reading. It was no longer the India we had inherited from Gandhi. That name stopped me like the striking of a match; suddenly revealing what 'G1', 'G2', 'G3', etc. stood for. It was yet another book about Gandhi then? If that was the case, I shouldn't have been surprised by it, but I was.

The outcome of the election in Bhopal a year earlier had stung Munna, even though the election pundits had predicted it. They had argued that the highest leader's positive image would carry even the most outrageous candidate of the ruling party to success. Hence, there was no reason that the Bhopal candidate's involvement in problematic activities would stop such a person from representing the city. But this argument did not suffice to explain the huge margin of the victory. Munna was personally hurt because he had strong associations with the city. But perhaps the other reason he felt so stunned had to do with the candidate's public avowal of admiration for Mahatma Gandhi's assassin. Even by the standards of the ruling party, this was a step too far.

As they routinely did in such cases, party leaders distanced themselves from the Bhopal candidate's comment, declaring it to be his personal view. The highest leader too had joined these leaders by remarking that he would never forgive such transgression. Forgive what, one might ask—for an appreciation of the murderer, or because the remark had revealed the party's long-held view? Of course, it was impossible to draw out this conclusion as the leader never amplified what he had pithily stated. No journalist dared ask him any question, and in any case, there was no occasion such as a press conference at which to do so. Five years had passed without his enduring a single such ritual of democracy. But on the matter of Gandhi's murder, the party and its numerous affiliates had maintained a safe, clever line for decades. Not only had they succeeded in dissociating the murderer from their ideology, but also their dissociation found acceptance in the official view expressed in school textbooks. Ever since Gandhi's murder, they described the perpetrator as a 'Hindu fanatic', thus avoiding any reference to the fact that he was ideologically committed to the hegemonic doctrine of Hindu nationalism.

The shock Munna felt on hearing the outcome of the election in Bhopal had first resulted in illness and then in depression. He had emerged from it, I thought, by distracting himself, travelling to America and then by starting to write a book. If this book was about Gandhi, it wouldn't have surprised me, but it didn't excite me either. Munna was no scholar, but he would have known that hundreds of books exist on Gandhi, illuminating every corner of his life that had no room for privacy. His 150th birth anniversary year, which had ended just a few months earlier, had brought a spate of new books, documents and annotated editions of his own writings. Some of the annotations were quite remarkable in their trivial pursuit of the variation in translations overseen by Gandhi himself—of his autobiography and the celebrated pamphlet *Hind Swaraj*. I doubt if Shakespeare had been subjected to such nitpicking over choice of phrase and spelling. Parallel to this, the ruling party had gone full blast to demonstrate its loyalty to the Mahatma. Its leaders saw great tourism potential in the various spots associated with Gandhi, particularly in Gujarat.

Old Gandhians, who had looked after institutions he had set up, found themselves being eased out one by one, to allow their roles to be taken over by new, qualified, managerial geniuses who believed in garish paints and flashing lights. They had already transformed the Sabarmati River in Ahmedabad into a scenic driveway to the airport, like a wannabe Shanghai.

It was beginning to make sense to me why Munna wanted to write a book about Gandhi—not so much on the historical Gandhi perhaps, but about the one who had inspired him as a child and changed him from being a royal to being a dedicated officer of free India. For the first time since opening Munna's files, I felt curious to find out everything about them. The sense of a difficult responsibility entrusted to me melted into a mellow feeling. Munna had perhaps tried and succeeded in expressing the sense of outrage that I had wanted to express myself. And why only me? A lot of people, who write regularly for the press and publish long commentaries, had strangely simmered down over recent years, becoming tame and trivial. No visible hand had seized their throat or gripped their wrist. No criminal investigation had been initiated to scare and silence them, nor did they have the kind of incomes that might attract the attention of the enforcement wing, prompting a review of tax returns. And yet, they had learned to hold back their sting. The more popular newspapers had stopped carrying any direct critical commentary. The so-called liberal voices had turned into bloggers, to be read by ardent followers rather than the public. It was a sinister transformation of the national ethos and many people my age had begun muttering among themselves that this was not the country they were born into. Surely, Munna had felt like that for a long time before the evening, when he learned of the Bhopal result. His terrible agitation and the subsequent stroke indicated that he must have felt throttled. Now that he was no longer there to face the consequences of speaking out freely, he was messaging me that he had finally decided to speak out, in these files.

It would be gratifying indeed to discover that he had cried for his beloved country with a sense of confidence about telling the truth. That he had found shelter in Gandhi looked so great that I felt a bit envious because I had felt quite shelter-less for several years now, with many a truth buried in my heart that I had been waiting to unveil in a more secure environment. The election due in 2019 had aroused the hope in my mind that change was inevitable. When it didn't happen, I had to accept the absence of any immediate relief from the wordless oppression that was now being practiced in the name of public policy. That Munna had spoken and left with me his writings now looked more inspiring rather than burdensome, as it had seemed only a day earlier. Such flip-flops of mood were not unique to me alone, although I was accustomed to living a life of such moody swings. Munna's manuscript would probably give me some therapeutic help, I now felt, as I resolved to open all the files the next day.

When I did that, I found myself buried under an avalanche. Each file dealt with both reality and memory, personal as well as public. Two of the files were in Hindi, steeped in a discourse that I instantly knew would be hard to convey in translation. Then there was a file containing sketches of individuals, some of whom I had met and known. How Munna had accommodated them in a book about Gandhi was difficult to guess. I would have to wait—and be patient—while reading the entire text, I told myself, to find out whether Munna had had an overall design for this book in mind, or had he just left it to me to tidy it all up and then pull it together.

As the afternoon of that hot and dusty day in May went by, I began to feel quite inadequate for the task; and not a little bit sorry for myself that I could hardly ignore it and

carry on living my life as if Munna's final email had not come
into my inbox. Had he simply died, I would have missed
him during the years to come, but that wouldn't have been
as hard as this gnawing realization that I had to work on this
scattered and potentially risky text and make it presentable
without making too many compromises with its spirit. I was
swimming in these vague, at times mortifying thoughts about
my own capacities and my friend's confidence in me when I
clicked open 'G8', the last file, which quickly showed that it
was the shortest and also different from the rest because it had
a title, 'Thank you, Gandhi'.

This title instantly gave me some clue about what Munna
had aspired to accomplish in his first ever venture into the world
of public writing. And perhaps he had achieved it, despite his
career in the civil service which had naturally imposed on him
the compulsion of never expressing his own thoughts or opinion
in any public media. I'm not saying that he was unaware of
the subtle art of suppressing the truth that the government had
mastered over the recent years. In fact, we had often discussed
it and exchanged our interpretation of how the growing rarity
of candour in the second decade of the twenty-first century
was different from the Emergency of the mid 1970s, that we
had both lived through as young adults. One thing was self-
evident—the difference between the character and style of
India's top leaders in 1975 and now. The leader at that time
was a sophisticated and beleaguered woman who had used
crude instruments like press censorship and mass incarceration
of opponents to consolidate her power. The leadership now had
no claim to subtlety but apparently knew how to avoid heavy-
handed tactics associated with fear. The owners of various
media houses themselves actively killed stories and thoughts
that might embarrass the government. Some television channels
were fully sold out, but some were not, creating evidence that

there was room for criticism, that the regime did tolerate free speech, especially that of a handful of reputed liberals. Some of these had been edged out of the print media by their own patron editors, and they now inhabited the virtual world of blogs and videos.

As children of a different era, Munna and I had shared our depressive thoughts numerous times over the telephone and in conversations after dinner, but this past year was different. What happened to him after the Bhopal election result was no mere shock. In fact, the shock had already set in when the candidacy of the ultimately victorious party was made public. It was an unabashed, teeth-grinding gesture of the ruling party, demonstrating how serious it was now, in its second term, to vanquish India's legacy of its struggle for its independence. Munna and I had grown up under the benign, extended shadow of that struggle and that of its leaders—Gandhi, Nehru and hundreds of others, including many in our own little hometown. The ruling party's choice for Bhopal had conveyed the message that the time had come for people like us to stop taking Gandhi and Nehru so seriously. One had been murdered and the other was now going to meet a similar posthumous fate. In the new world, we had unwittingly entered in the last phases of our lives, we had no choice left. But as I soon discovered, these were not the thoughts and feelings that 'G8' contained.

The text in this file was a complete surprise. Its crisp brevity reflected a man who had conquered despair and regained his hold on the thread that had nearly slipped out of his shaky hands on to the floor when the house had descended into darkness in a power failure. The text of 'G8' showed that Munna saw his life as a coherent whole, rejecting the fracture others had accepted to live with. I read this file to the last line and for more than a few moments I felt relief blowing through my heart like a breeze, the relief that it was not a political book after

all that my friend had asked me to look after as his statement
to a politically cursed country. Even as this consoling thought
passed through my mind, I kicked myself with a degree of self-
derision for being so self-centred and task-oriented. How could
I look at this task merely as a copy editor's responsibility to
adjust a manuscript to the times? Munna's trauma demanded
justice, exacting the price that justice always demands.

I nudged myself back into the reality of my own inner
world. Munna's memory and writing, which I had still not fully
read for fear of the scale of the difficulties that it might bring
upon me if I did justice to it, goaded me hard. It was difficult
to judge in which direction it was goading me. After all, he was
an intimate, loving friend who could never think of pushing
me into things I could not cope with. Alive or not, he would
be the first person to know that threats and legal troubles were
beyond my capacities to manage. That had been the case all
my life although I was the son of a criminal lawyer who had
specialized in cases of dacoity and murder. As for Munna, in
the initial period of his career, he had served the government
in the violent jungles of what is now Chhattisgarh (formerly a
part of Madhya Pradesh) without selling his soul to the devil
of the state and its fascination with the maintenance of law and
order no matter how much human misery it incurred. That was
the way when the British were here, and it was no different
now, Munna had said many times. Some of the instances he
used to state to prove his point were from his experience in the
aftermath of the Bhopal gas tragedy. I hadn't yet read the Hindi
file in which I had assumed he would deal with this part of his
experience, but I knew from numerous conversations with him
that handling the ravages of the Union Carbide leak in Bhopal
included the muzzling of truth and editing of ghastly experiences
of thousands of poor people so that everything could be neatly
adjusted in the grand narrative of the government.

My mind was all over the place. It remained like that—confused and perplexed—for several days and nights. At times, I felt weighed down by the burden of responsibility that I wasn't sure I could carry without feeling that I would put myself into trouble. At other times, I felt touched by my old friend's trust in me and my capacity to tell his story. I couldn't help being reminded of Horatio in *Hamlet*. When Shakespeare's tragic play ends and the stage is littered with corpses, Hamlet asks Horatio to stay alive to tell 'his' story. Hamlet, on the brink of death, realizes that the story of his life and approaching end are not easy to fit into a sensible narrative and Horatio also knows that well, because nothing has changed in the world that had deeply disturbed Hamlet. A single line from the earlier part of the play captures it all: 'Something is rotten in the State of Denmark.' If one put 'India' in place of Denmark in that line, it would be an apt description of the second decade of the twenty-first century. Although I had not yet read right through the files Munna had sent me, except for the last one, 'G8', I dreaded the risk that I would have to run if I brought into the public space the descriptions of the rot that I was sure I would find in different files.

Suddenly, a clever idea occurred to me on how to proceed. 'G8' had hardly any direct reference to politics or to the assault on democracy and its values. This brief file was almost purely psychological, verging on the spiritual. It conveyed Munna's gratitude to a source of energy and continuity that he had felt lucky to have enjoyed right to the end of his life. The sentiments, evoked by expressing gratitude to Gandhi, were steeped in philosophy, or rather in philosophical identification. Couldn't I pick up phrases and sentences from this file and disperse them throughout the book, to take the edges off specific references and discussions on men in power who had destroyed all possibility of truth being spoken? Their handy

violence and vindictiveness could perhaps be offset with the
help of a literary cloud.

And what would that do to my late friend's yearning
to accomplish something he had never done earlier in his
life—to write in order to tell the truth? By clever editing and
reassembling, I might succeed in making his book appear less
strident, easier to publish, but is that why he left it with me, I
asked myself. What was I afraid of if I owned the book, wrote
a foreword for it, approving its perspective and the facts used
in it to indict a regime that has entertained every intention
of co-opting Gandhi and burying him for good. I reminded
myself that I hadn't actually read the full text. If I did and
then decided what to do, I might feel less frantic and less
haunted by prospects that might not be real at all. This was
clearly a saner thought, arising from the depths of my own
unacknowledged depression that had been building up for
several years or perhaps longer.

All available paths of talking or writing about India's loss of
its own self, which I and my friend's generation had identified
with, had been closed off one by one. The youngsters studying
in colleges and universities had no idea of the anguish and
disappointment of our generation. They had ceased to resist
and protest, and those few among them who had the temerity
to protest had ended up in jail after brazenly false charges were
levelled against them. The Nehru University student leader,
Keshav Kishor, had been charged with sedition. Another
student leader had her head smashed, and more recently, two
young women, Devaki and Nutan, had been thrown into jail,
to wait for trial along with several of their feminist colleagues
for inciting the Delhi riots. This was a preposterous India
where nothing aroused official conscience or public ire even
among the youth. This was a new country where no one cared
if an innocent voice was muzzled, and anyone associated with

it was put away for a few years until his or her spirit fully broke. This was a country that had agreed to be run by a techno-moral regime with an unabashed capacity to use fear as the means of routine control. Having perceived this root cause of the pervasive paralysis of conscience I had felt surrounded by for years, I felt strangely relieved and refreshed. I was ready to peruse all the files Munna had sent me with care and determination—to do my best to enable his voice to get the audience it deserved.

Though I remembered next morning what I had decided, it took me almost a week to start reading. Instead of starting with the first file as I had thought I would, I opened the two Hindi files. I had somehow anticipated that it would be in the text of these files that Munna would have poured out his deeper thoughts without the effort of having to write in English. Neither of us had learned English in our early years. Munna learned it in Scindia when he was already thirteen. My school wasn't as capable of compensating for the lack of early exposure as the institutions Munna attended were. And while we both became competent in English later on; it never acquired the power to express our emotions. Our relationship remained dependent on the language that our parents and neighbours spoke and which our first teachers in the school at Kundeshwar taught us to read and write. I was sure that 'G5' and 'G6', the two files composed in Hindi, would give me the view of Munna's mind in his last few months that I needed, to understand and work on his manuscript. As it turned out, both the Hindi files were mostly about Bhopal. The first one dealt with its rise and fall as a modern city, from its glorious beginnings as the capital of Madhya Pradesh to the catastrophe brought upon it by an American pesticide company. The second file was similar in its landscape. It covered the decline of Bhopal, from a city where peace had prevailed between Muslims and Hindus despite

the Partition storm, to becoming the crucible of a long-term
experiment of the Hindu nationalist zealots to create lasting
discord and hatred.

There were several overlaps between the text these two
Hindi files contained. In one of these overlapping portions,
Munna had drawn a connection between Bhopal's loss of
social heritage and the accident it had suffered. The link he
had tried to establish reminded me of the broken lines we
used as school children to indicate the presence of water in
our pencil drawings. The broken lines and what they stood for
were a matter of artistic convention on our part. As children
often do, we didn't think about it. Munna had referred to
Gandhi and his view about disasters having moral origins.
In Hindi, the point did not look as awkward as it would in
English, I thought, and it occurred to me that English has
a certain matter-of-fact crispness as a language. Hindi, on
the other hand, had a certain imaginative vagueness which
carried the promise of protection from being fully understood
by evil-minded people. Perhaps Munna was aware of this
difference and was therefore experimenting with the two
languages.

When he started writing the book, the protest waged at
Shaheen Bagh in South Delhi by Muslim women against the
CAA had changed the ethos of Delhi. Their protest had the
effect of sudden rain brought by a western disturbance to a
city choked by pollution and humidity: it revived confidence
and energy in the exhausted inhabitants. The hope invoked by
Shaheen Bagh must have made Munna feel bolder about what
he could get away with in his book. I was sure that the Bhopal
chapters, separate but tenuously connected, with repetitions
and overlaps, were compositions of that brief period. Would a
translation from Hindi into English convey that subtle influence
of the anti-CAA campaign?

Before I started to wonder about that, yet another doubt started to nag me: wouldn't a translation seem like a fracture and make the book awkward? I would have to rewrite the Bhopal portion, I told myself somewhat nervously. Also, I reminded myself, Munna's reference to Gandhi's faith in the moral origins of natural disasters would have to be explained—and not just explained but would have to be justified with suitable commentary that would make Gandhi look rational. Moreover, the relevance of Gandhi's idea in the context of an industrial disaster would have to be established, as a logical extension of the original idea, one which even Tagore had found difficult to swallow. Many recent books on Gandhi had tried to do just that. His religiosity had been accepted long ago, but it didn't cover all his angular eccentricities. Whereas earlier biographers had simply accepted who he was—and some like James Vincent Sheean respected and were comfortable with the most irksome eccentricities—the new biographers had spared no effort to refurbish Gandhi's known personality and turn him into a liberal rationalist. The effort was painstaking and didn't work in all contexts, so a lot of editing was done to make Gandhi marketable. I shuddered at the thought that I too might have to do just that—if I found that Munna had portrayed Gandhi's views with acceptance of the arcane in him.

This is exactly what I did find in two of the files. These dealt with village life and rural development. 'G2' contained an elaborate section where Munna had reminisced about the government's policies to alleviate village backwardness and strategies for removing it. The discussion showed how intimately Munna had participated in these policies, while maintaining serious doubts about their efficacy and intentions. It was hard to say whether he had cultivated these doubts after his retirement as many officers do. The prose did not give me convincing proof one way or the other. At one point, Munna had articulated a memory of the mortification he had felt on account of the compulsions he had to work under. As if he had become aware of this problem as a writer, he returned to it in 'G3' when he dealt with the least defensible of all of Gandhi's bizarre ideas—the ones on doctors, lawyers, the railways and parliamentary democracy in *Hind Swaraj*.

Even Nehru found this tract embarrassing and unacceptable. *Hind Swaraj* had remained an undisputable proof that Gandhi was a misfit in any frame of rationalism or even reasonable progressivism. Despite the criticism that some of his closest friends and admirers expressed, Gandhi stuck to the positions he had taken in *Hind Swaraj* that the critics had described as 'absurd'. He had written it when he was quite young, but he reiterated his commitment to everything he had written in this bizarre booklet. Even today, Gandhi's views on health, technology and representative democracy sound incredibly strange. Munna had acknowledged this, but at the same time he had endorsed Gandhi's outlook and polemic that formed the basic structure of *Hind Swaraj*. But that didn't worry me in the least because no one now takes Gandhi's perspective on doctors and railways seriously. Even his general perception of modern technology arouses no interest: it is simply ignored and dismissed with a smirk. Munna had extended Gandhi's critique of technology to the current sway of digital devices and had not spared the prime minister's pet dream of Digital India. But the risk involved in such daring criticism was nothing compared to what lay in 'G7' and 'G8' for me to discover.

These two files went into the fascination that Hindu nationalist stalwarts and organizations had felt for fascism when it arose in Germany and Italy. I was quite surprised to find that Munna had delved into both the history and the cultural geography, so to say, of his fascination. Apparently, he had thought a great deal about this, supplementing his reflections with study of the 1920s and the 1930s in central and western India. Given how much space Munna had devoted to narrating the known details of Gandhi's assassination, it made sense that he dwelt on the network of Hindu nationalist groups and institutions. However, the concern mirrored in this discussion had a piercing character to it, suggestive of a personal wound.

As far as I knew or remembered, Munna could have had no history of direct experience with any Hindu majoritarian outfit. But it was naïve of me to think that I knew Munna's life in sufficient detail, to be aware of his different kinds of encounters with communal organizations and the ubiquitous aggression they permit themselves from time to time. In Madhya Pradesh, where Munna had served as an officer for the longest part of his administrative career, Hindu communal outfits had a considerable record of what can only be called casually perpetrated violence. It's as if you do something short, sharp and nasty, then you deny it and publicly wash your hands of it, then you do it again and follow it up with more hand washing so routinely that your critics prefer to stay in permanent confusion and uncertainty about your real character. The same holds true for the police, who find themselves equally confused. This was an Indian version of what the German and Italian youth groups had practiced during the 1930s.

Munna had drawn a large contour—with several receding contour lines accommodated within it—to describe the culture of violence, permanent aggression and anger directed at Gandhi. Sustainable or not from a historical point of view, this portraiture would be sufficient to make Munna's book irritating and unacceptably annoying for those enjoying dominance in the present moment, I thought.

The history of youth activism associated with the ideology of religious nationalism is consistent with the behaviour of the political masters. They perceive sporadic punitive action as a necessary and legitimate resource to remind people that they exist and aspire. They don't take criticism lightly or as part of the game of public life. Especially now when they have tasted power and have enjoyed it, they find a certain pleasure in showing to the reluctant that they will not let a critic go without retribution even if he is no more. They are heartless chasers of power, and they don't believe in letting anything go or heal. I could well imagine them putting pressure on or harassing Munna's wife or daughters, demanding the withdrawal of his book. No matter how carefully I might cleanse it of corrosive material, its publication in the current and impending time would pose the risk of trouble for Munna's family.

An alternative course of action seemed worth considering, and before long, it seemed the right thing to do. Munna had sent me this material when he felt that he might not be able to complete what he had started. Barring the two files about Bhopal, which, as I have said, were composed in Hindi, the rest were not merely incomplete: they were like scattered notes, passionate and deep, here and there, but almost like jottings at other places, set down to remind the writer that more was required here. There were countless gaps, some of them indicated by one or two short phrases showing the kind of bridging text needed to convey the continuity of an idea. Gandhi's presence pervaded many parts of the text, but at many points it was more like the invocation of somebody you miss. An emotional poignancy is perhaps what Munna was trying to achieve, as if he was attempting to spread all over the book the sting that Bhopal's election of its representative in Parliament had given him.

During some of my conversations with him in the weeks following the 2019 election, I had wondered why I had not been stung as sharply as he had been by the news about Bhopal, why that sense of instant gloom stemming from the totality of loss had spared my mind and heart. Perhaps it was because Munna felt closer to Bhopal. He had served there—in good times and bad. Or perhaps, my sensibility had been eroded by cynicism and cowardice. It was true that Munna had stayed clear of cynicism despite having spent his life in the bureaucracy. The files offered no clue. He had composed these files without letting anyone know what they contained. All I knew was that he was writing something in those months, but even I didn't know *what* he was writing. There was no doubt in my mind that he had emailed these files to me in confidence, days before his death. There was no way to determine, and it would not be worth the trouble to try, whether he had deleted and destroyed the files after mailing them to me, probably along with a lot of other things that his computer had accumulated over the years as everybody's does.

The message in his email, to which the files had been attached, set out a task that, on the surface, looked like the unfinished work a dying man did not want to see go to waste. The meaning of that message depended on what one thought that work was—its nature and the personal logic it would be guided by in the mind of the receiver of the message. Now that I had gone through all the files, even if cursorily, I had felt more than once somewhat envious of my late and intimate friend.

It's strange that I should call it envy. At our school, he was a class ahead of me, so there was never any question of competition for a teacher's attention or appreciation or higher grades. It was a basic school where craftwork, as Gandhiji had proposed, was the core curriculum. All children learned to work on clay, cotton, papier mâché, wood and such things. We were free to work at our own pace and were repeatedly told to work for our own satisfaction and pleasure. Every few weeks, the teacher asked us to carry one of the objects we had made by hand, to show to our parents. On Diwali, we were told to select what we thought were among our best-made artefacts. I can't recall the year, but I am sure it was not either my or Munna's final year in that school. Our Diwali vacation was not as long as it was in other schools, but it did start a week before the festival. Sitting in his car at the end of the school day to go home, I showed a painted clay doll I had chosen to show to my mother, and I asked Munna what he had chosen. He took out from his bag a small, square, somewhat rough handkerchief. Its hemming was not quite straight, but in the middle there were three interlocking embroidered circles in different colours. I found it strange that Munna should have chosen something like that as his best work, because I thought, though my teacher had pushed me hard to abandon the idea, that stitching and embroidery were girls' work. And that's exactly what, as Munna told me when he came to my home later that evening, his father had said on seeing the handkerchief.

That day stands out in my mind as the only occasion when I felt jealous of Munna. He always showed everything he made to my mother, and that evening he gifted her the handkerchief. My mother was visibly touched and she praised the quality of the weaving, hemming and embroidery, lightly touching the stitches with her fingers. Envy stung me sharply that day. The doll I had made with great care now seemed childish, compared to Munna's hanky, and I kicked myself for not having thought of something more useful than a clay doll. The envy that Munna's Gandhi files made me feel for a passing moment had no such sting or bite whatsoever, it was just a faint reminder, barely audible in the mind—a reminder of something I had let go of and Munna had not. That something—call it a child's integrity—was worth redeeming. In a flash of insightful self-awareness, I knew exactly what to do. The project he had embarked on in the Gandhi files was so incomplete that it could at best be described as a sketch of what he had had in mind. I would make it a joint project, to save myself while it was still possible to do so.

For a day or so I remained in a limbo, not able to decide whether I was reading far too much into Munna's last email. The rival thought was that I had come to the right conclusion, both about what that message signified and what best I could do with Munna's porous manuscript. It was porous in the sense that I could find myself in many of its vacant spaces. The manner in which I would fill in those spaces seemed like a great and opportune assignment that Munna had, perhaps inadvertently, given me, to resurrect myself as his childhood friend. In the following days, the envy that I have tried to describe became centred itself in the feeling that Munna had lived and died without surrendering the child in him under the suffocating pressure of gloomy circumstances and shady rulers. He had remained loyal to the country we had grown up in at its dawn.

Having passed through a prolonged struggle in a pitch-dark night in the moment of its birth, the country had gifted us a lovely, orange-coloured dawn and a cool breeze coming through the windows of an old car as it drove past ancient mahua trees releasing their gently intoxicating scent. Was it the country or was it the frail figure of an old man who had left behind a thousand good ideas for us and for humanity before getting shot three times in the chest for his good deeds? Munna had found in him a medicine to get rid of his despair. I had surrendered to that despair but hadn't known it. It was the preliminary reading of Munna's files and the memory of our telephone conversations during the days of the Shaheen Bagh protests and the Delhi riots that reminded me and ultimately enabled me to recognize the mutated face of that despair—apathy.

Apathy tells you that if there's nothing you can do about something, then it's alright to do nothing about everything.

Dante's visit to hell starts with the recognition of apathy as the most common condition in the human population. People spend their lives without taking sides. They notice evil but lack the energy to resist it. Munna had served in many government posts, and in each of them he had found some way to act for whatever good was possible. As for me, having been a teacher for most of my life, a writer, and having briefly served in a powerful position, I had developed a personal theory that your good ideas matter only if you are in a position to carry them through. The contrast between the lives Munna and I had led revealed to me a hidden weakness of mine. It lay in my narrow way of treating that word—position.

This revelation, true or not, had a magical effect. Though he had died, Munna had put me in the position to join him in telling the truth. We had witnessed and felt in our hearts the loss of the gains that the country that we had believed in had suffered. The country had made these gains under Gandhi's unique presence and leadership. The gains were not lost all at once. As children we had enjoyed these gains without the understanding of what we had learned early to enjoy. It was a sense of coherence in our lives, and Munna's text was nothing but a faltering attempt to celebrate that coherence and to express gratitude for it to Gandhi. The text was now inviting me to own it, become a part of it. It wanted me to weigh the risks involved in telling the world truthfully what all had happened in recent years—to change the world that our teachers had initiated us into, transferring their own uncanny energy in the process.

I went to Munna's house and asked Pushpa to show me his collection of books on Gandhi. I thought I must go through some of the books Munna had read to be able to do justice to the text he had left behind. Some of the titles were predictable, like Louis Fischer's biography and the Tendulkar volumes.

Then there were others that I had heard of but hadn't read, like Erik Erikson's *Gandhi's Truth* and Sudhir Kakar's *Mira and the Mahatma*. It took me months to catch up with Munna's readings, and I am not sure that I actually did.

Nearly all the texts I picked up to read initially conveyed an echo of familiarity. What I had known about Gandhi soon appeared like an obstacle. This happened most strikingly when I reread the parts of his autobiography that I was fully acquainted with. I began to think that the current political context was making it difficult for me to feel comfortable. Is Gandhi relevant at all? It popped up as a nagging question every time I paid attention to the lucidity of his style and the transparency of his arguments. Surely these qualities were important and had to be respected particularly because Gandhi was a politician, but they sustained my uncertainty about engaging with Munna's text. Gandhi's words offered no obvious bridge between what appeared to be his simplicity and the meanings that seemed to lurk under the surface of Munna's text. Munna had discussed at great length the many possible connotations that 'truth' carried for Gandhi. This discussion was full of gaps, indicated at many spots by dots. Perhaps he had expected to fill in these gaps later. How would I deal with them, I anxiously wondered. Deletion was the easy option; filling up presented an unattractive challenge, for it would involve reading a whole lot more of, and on, Gandhi than I would have wanted to. If Munna had left some handwritten notes that might help me, perhaps Pushpa could find them, I thought, but I didn't have the heart to ask her. Her grief was greater than mine; it was better to leave her alone.

One such essay on Gandhi's death is by Vincent Sheean; unfortunately, it is filled with so much personal devotion and determination to learn directly from Gandhi the secret of his energy and sense of purpose, that an ordinary reader cannot go beyond feeling mesmerized. That's why, I suppose, I had greater appreciation for the essays written upon hearing the news of Gandhi's murder by the American novelist, Mary McCarthy and the British political thinker and writer George Orwell. It's in Mary McCarthy's essay that one realizes the meaning of murder as a way of ending someone's life. McCarthy does not mention Godse, and in all likelihood she was not aware of the depth of Godse's hatred for Gandhi. Nor did she know much about the ideology that translated, in the minds of Godse and his team, into the desire to shoot Gandhi dead. Mary McCarthy focuses on the ease of killing.

Reading her essay, one recognizes the contrast between the long, slowly lived life of Gandhi and its quick ending. It's all fragile—Mary McCarthy seems to say about the story of greatness and veneration, not to mention love, that Gandhi is supposed to have enjoyed. Of course it's true. If any more evidence other than Gandhi's political success was needed, it came in his funeral procession. Famous descriptions exist, showing tens of thousands of men and women breaking down. These descriptions are silent about the murder: even the long eyewitness account of the funeral procession broadcast on All India Radio on 31 January 1948, the day following the murder, doesn't mention a word about the assassination and why it occurred. The ease of violence that Mary McCarthy mentions had spread far and wide. Only an American could have felt that ease being a problem as she did. We Indians don't even like to remember it although the police, the lawyers, the judge and the government of the day did their job and hanged Godse as soon as possible. One wonders if Godse's fame would have suffered, at least in the long run, had he been given life imprisonment instead of the death sentence. In the annals of killing, a life spent in prison would have dwarfed him and his followers. Sparing his life would also have pleased Gandhi. Revenge killing by the State hardly matched his ideals.

Another famous essay that I read, by George Orwell, fed me a different kind of food by rejecting the idea that Gandhi was a humanist. Someone so spiritual and driven by religiosity, Orwell wrote, cannot be called a humanist. These were strong words. No wonder they arouse controversy even seventy years later. Those who like to think that liberal humanism is the best bulwark against the ideology of religious nationalism and majoritarianism rampant in today's Indian politics feel that Orwell was wrong. Proving that Gandhi was liberal is not particularly hard. The same is true of efforts to prove that he was secular. These terms are the popular weapons of modernists. That Gandhi doesn't fit neatly in the accepted frame of modernity is common knowledge, and liberal humanism poses similar issues; therefore, Orwell was not all that wrong when he argued that Gandhi's saintly piety was incompatible with the political philosophy of a human-centric vision of progress.

Orwell did not deny Gandhi the tallest stature among his contemporary leaders in the world. But creating a doubt about Gandhi's humanism does hurt. One would like to use Gandhi to fight the battle we are in against religious hatred and divisive politics, but it looks difficult to do so without ignoring Gandhi's grave scepticism about the kind of progress that a modern economy and State offer. It's a conundrum. You cannot sort it out by reasoning alone. There is something else that one needs, and that's what Munna had found in the darkness that surrounded him in the summer of 2019. The short tenth file called 'Thank you, Gandhi', indicated that Munna was seeking sustenance from a saint when all other sources had run dry.

I had read this short file twice a few weeks earlier, but this time when I reread it, it came across as if it had been composed as a letter written by a child or perhaps an adolescent. The sentences were short, and the words exuded the urge on the part of the writer to conceal deep depression. Submission to a moral authority surfaced here and there, but there was no hiding the powerless rage of a child. Although the text was scattered and far from being organized, its emotive content was like that of Mary McCarthy's. How can the world be so cynical that it could carry right on, she had asked when her colleagues heard the news of Gandhi's murder without interrupting their meal, as if it was a part of a normal day? How could one not be grateful to someone like Gandhi for just living? Munna's note of gratitude to Gandhi had exactly that tone, but with one difference. Mary McCarthy was worried about the world whereas Munna's worry was centred on India. Reading those three pages, I felt both scared and reassured—as if the emotions, which I had done my best to conceal when the current immoral regime had come to power, had now become known to me through my old friend's prose.

We had been friends since childhood; Munna had sustained that childhood and its sanctity till the last months of his well-lived life. His words made me shudder for the loss of my childhood, or rather, its sanctity, suggesting that I had allowed it to be wounded by not worrying as much as he had about the loss that he had described in the files he had sent me before dying. These were notes he was inviting me to complete, but I had first to join him. If I were to add to his text, then I would have to find a means of distinguishing my insertions from the original manuscript. I had to treat this as our book, a sacred celebration of the times in which we were born and had been blessed to grow up in. It was clear that my friend was asking me to shed my cynicism and fear. What was the point of my being a writer if I merely refined my friend's text, so that it would satisfy some ho-hum publisher? He was no longer there to have to worry about the consequences of telling the truth.

This liberation had rightly selected Gandhi as its symbol. This was not the historical Gandhi, it was a saint whom one might invoke, pray to, and thank for dispelling gloom and anxiety.

My decision to hold Gandhi in my mind in this manner had an instant, releasing impact. I felt free from the bondage of Gandhi's biographers, memoirists and scholars. I felt free of the Gandhi industry which stands as polarized in today's India as do politics and society. The Gandhi industry is also in charge of managing the chicanery necessary for those committed to being hostile towards Gandhi since their childhood. They've always hated Gandhi, but they realize that they need him to maintain their grip on power. Using Gandhi for tourism is a minor sin compared to his being accommodated in their pantheon. Gandhi, the politician who dealt with the men who adorn the pantheon, is long dead. Why should I worry about that Gandhi? Munna didn't. If I were now to collaborate with him in completing his book, treating it also as my own, I must get rid of all traces of the desire I have routinely felt as a writer to remain authentic and reliable as a source of knowledge.

Once I have conceded Gandhi's sainthood, I told myself, I am at liberty to relate to him with freedom and confidence. Munna had already started to walk along this pathway, interpreting truth, violence and non-violence, and the rest of the Gandhi staple, in his own way. Let me enjoy the same freedom in the insertions that I would compose in order to fill in the numerous gaps that Munna had indicated by dots. This decision also provided me with the intellectual security that I had missed over recent years. Witnessing the gradual loss of confidence among stalwarts had forced me to stay cool and acquiescent in the brave new ethos of the country.

The procedure for working on the manuscript became clear and started to unfold. Except for one file, I felt I need not restrain my hand too much while extending Munna's text. It was going to be necessary to reorganize the files, and that would require dispersing their contents into chapters. In many places, Munna had referred to me by name. I let these portions stay as they were, except for changing my name to 'K.'. To fill in the gaps he had left, I elaborated his text, trying my best to keep the style intact, using the spaces for an on-going conversation between us and the reader.

I let his description of Bhopal stay. It was his Bhopal; he knew it inside-out. All I had to do with his Bhopal notes was to translate them from Hindi. This might not be difficult, but it actually turned out to be just as much of a challenge as working with my friend on the rest of the files. These decisions boosted my confidence that Gandhi and Munna would end a state of mind that permitted little room for hope of witnessing a political turn-around within my remaining lifetime.

This was no mere escape from the gloom that had surrounded Munna in his final months. I have already written the question he had asked me, in a rare display of desperation: 'Will they destroy everything?' No, what I now felt could not be termed an escape from such thoughts. Rather, it was a revival of spirit to continue to believe that things will emerge from the grip of a false truth and a fallible imagination engineered by democratic procedures. I felt released and ready to devote myself to a new, shining purpose. If life means pursuing a purpose that seems consistent with the ones you have been pursuing so far, I had one in my hand.

PART TWO

Munna's Text, with K.'s Inserts

I

Will Gandhi's idea of truth help me cope with the pain and stress I suffer each day as a witness to relentless defacing of the India I grew up in? I am not used to seeing videos showing scenes of lynching or someone tied with a chain being dragged by a car. Everywhere I look, there is fear of violence. Those who agree with the dominant ideology want to redefine India's selfhood. They think the public has given them the mandate to do so. They seek their justification from their old ideological masters and present-day leaders. They display their collective might wherever they choose—changing names of cities and villages, roads, shifting and damaging museum objects, destroying old buildings and institutions, and altering the textbooks that children study at school. Their rude disregard for the past is spreading like a plague. At times, when I find myself sick with depression at the thought that my life was wasted, I try to regain balance by imagining that Gandhi might have had similar thoughts at several junctures in his life, especially after the Partition. Every time I try to sort out my thoughts, I slip into shadows. I start again and when I feel stable, I believe

Gandhi must have helped me. I read him, about him, and then, at times, I find myself talking to him, seeking clarity, conveying my doubts and fears.

If you feel your world is crashing, then you know that you have lived much too long, I often tell myself. Quite a few people of my generation who have enjoyed success in professional public life have acknowledged that the country they were born in has metamorphosed. That country was in their mind; they lived their lives under the belief that their efforts would take the country closer to that mental image. Perhaps there is a better way to say this. In any case, it sounds more accurate to say that they treated the country they grew up in as their real country and didn't notice that it was changing all the time, slowly, imperceptibly, into something quite different, an ugly copy of itself. Let me correct myself: not everyone in my circle felt like that. Some calibrated their emotions to the changing scene, keeping their eyes open to the opportunities the new variant might offer. One or two grabbed the opportunities presented to them, without the fear or hesitation that the sense of an impending loss of dignity entails. Serving to facilitate the birth of the new version of our nation did not bother them, at least not publicly. They must have told themselves—their deeper answering service if one can call conscience by that name—that they were still serving the State, the same State that they were sworn to serve as part of the civil service. If the State had been grabbed by leaders who had little faith in the ideals of the Constitution, well that's their business, these friends of mine must have told themselves. That is why it didn't hurt them much now that the secular lyric they had sung in their long careers had begun to change, first the tune and then the words. I admire their agile ageing selves so much I can't even convey my revulsion.

That would be rude, and that is one thing my father had told me to try controlling whenever the impulse arose. A brother of the King, my father had no duties except to stay polite, even on occasions when one couldn't be kind. That ideal of behaviour I have found hard to shed. The Scindia School and Daly College reinforced it. Sometimes, I used to feel jealous of K., and of his easier life at a government school and college. He must be more relaxed there, where they probably left you alone to let your own resources grow, without worries about the School's template of conscience. I may be quite wrong and unjust, but I know K. never lost the conscience our primary school had asked us to preserve. Conscience may be out of fashion in the age of opportunity, but coherence will do for me. What exactly was conscience, I now wonder. Was it the same thing as 'aatmaa', the thing that sits deeper than the mind, in the mind? Translation helps figure out the distinction. In Hindi, 'aatmaa'—normally referred to in English as 'the soul'—would translate as one's defining 'self', whereas conscience is what makes one aware of how something is essentially, morally wrong. The self is the principle of coherence—that thread of life that stays straight, no matter how many turns life takes. It is a slender thread, capable of snapping if the valleys you go through are too deep. Our spinning teacher had taught us how to tie a tiny knot when the thread breaks despite your focus on the spindle and the piece of cotton in your right hand. What he did not teach was what to do when the thread breaks because you can't judge where you are. The evening I heard about the election outcome in Bhopal, I know I felt fully disoriented— even though I had prepared myself over the weeks for just that result. It was only much later that I was able rejoin the ends of my snapped thread, knotting them when I stumbled on Gandhi. While reading him I realized that the thread that had snapped in me was what he called truth.

A man can become a legislator by winning an election. To do so, he might use his innate qualities of leadership and follow the rules laid down for fighting an election. Then, when he has been elected, he ignores the real interests of the people who voted for him, because he only used them to bolster his political faction and its long-term agenda. This is hardly new. Time and again, and in many different countries, history shows that common people are easy to manipulate and mobilize, not because they are indifferent to politics or innocent, but simply because they are much too occupied with fighting the daily battle of life. They live in a world of others like themselves, and they don't realize that they count for little more than grist in the electoral mill of democracy. A seasoned orator can persuade them to kill someone who has done no wrong. It is easy to stir them up for causes they might have abhorred or at least, would never have thought of.

Shakespeare portrayed this characteristic of the masses in his play *Julius Caesar*, in the scene where Mark Antony persuades the common people of Rome to go after Brutus and Brutus's colleagues. A few hours earlier, these same people were pleased with Brutus for killing Caesar. All that Mark Antony had for redirecting them was the power of words, images and metaphors. His speech is a fine example of how populist public leaders target ordinary people's emotions, arousing and fanning them to the point of frenzy. Shaking out Caesar's cloak, Antony asks the people to look at the holes in it. These holes were made by the knives of Caesar's assassins, says Antony to the crowd assembled before him. Caesar's blood flowed through these holes, he says. Antony makes the murder of Caesar occur all over again, through his words, at a pace carefully measured to create frenzy.

That was a temporary frenzy, but people can be mobilized for sustainable insanity as well. That is what Hitler and his associates did in Germany. The demonic energy they released took the lives of six million Jews and tormented the whole world with a terrible war that ended in nuclear horror. How much misery was unleashed in this long episode of German democracy can hardly be calculated. Firm believers in parliamentary democracy get defensive when they are reminded of this history. Democracy is the best hope we have, they say with a sigh. Gandhi's criticism of the British parliamentary system in *Hind Swaraj* must have irritated them.

The parliamentary model rests on deference to the majority view. It is a crude notion, and that is why Gandhi disapproved of it. The idea that a numerical majority can decide things did not match his favourite totem—truth, a strange, elusive, almost funny word. It's funny because it takes so many forms, the way a magician conjures colours in the sky. Early at school one learns to call it 'the' truth—as if there is just one truth whereas lies are always many. I didn't know before entering college that when truth is under dispute, it is a lawyer's job to establish it. As a young boy, I was attracted to law because I had read that Gandhi and Nehru were lawyers before they became political leaders. It must be a great profession, I thought, but K.'s father, who was an eminent lawyer in our district, dissuaded me from studying law. You may work hard as a lawyer, he said, but you can't win a case if the judge has received a bribe. I was quite shocked when I first heard this, but later on when I joined the civil services, I understood why K.'s father had warned me against studying law. Soon after joining the civil services, I learnt how truth-hiding became, at times, as important as truth-seeking. As a small boy, I had seen the dead body of a dacoit, stretched out in the hockey ground of my home town. My elder sister had whispered in my ear: 'The minister wouldn't know . . . It's a farmer.' Her whisper made no sense for years; then, one day the meaning dawned on me, that liberties can be taken with the truth to impress a VIP.

'Truth' has proved to be the trickiest of all the values that Gandhi espoused for his enemies to dent or erase, but its meaning has been shifting all along. When young people today are told that Gandhi died for truth, they are puzzled. If they hear that a film is based on a true story, it is assumed that the story is real. When they watch something strange on the screen of their smartphone or television, how often do they stop to ask if it is real, I wonder. And who would they ask? They know that it might be fake, but how can anyone be sure of that? True or fake, it hardly matters so long as it is amusing. That is more important now than truth.

Gandhi's idea of truth was probably different. People rarely consider it necessary to explain it, but one of my primary school teachers did. He said, 'It meant the right way—one can call it goodness.' That left a lot of scope for confusion, I thought, much later. If truth is goodness, can a newspaper story be true or otherwise? An account of what is going on may be real or fiction. Perhaps my primary teacher and Gandhi meant that a story is true when the object of describing something has the potential to do some good. It helps to think like that, but it doesn't calm my present rage. My despair sits deep within me. My mind wanders. The Congress is paying for its various sins, but its vanquishers have exceeded all previous records of propagating falsehood. The 'facts' they flaunt about their achievements last a few weeks, mostly a few days before a lost soul challenges them. The figures given out for marking India's economic growth and prospects were dummies. The real figures had to wait for the long election spring and summer to pass. Slogans and promises don't sit well with truth, but the vast voting public didn't seem to mind.

I am surrounded by these falsehoods—and I am not a part of the so-called social media where fakery roams free. Day in and day out, I endure the untruth. It serves as a cover for hate—the real agenda of the new regime. What the British learnt to practice bit by bit—how to dig trenches between communities—

has swollen into the theatre of the grotesque. It is beamed every evening to every region of the waiting nation. It numbs and terrifies as you watch. Hating its actors and directors restores my sanity for a moment, but I can still hear myself talking as if I am deranged, to Gandhi.

'Is it all right to hate some people? Will you let me hate the men in power now?'

'So, you hate them . . . do you?'

'Yes, but I feel you will not be pleased . . . You never hated anyone it seems. Is that true?'

'I tried not to.'

'I also try but I don't succeed.'

'You must ask yourself why you don't.'

'That's easy . . . My hatred helps me control my despair. Don't you think it's a tough choice?'

'You've changed the question. I was asking you to find the root of your hatred, not how it helps you.'

'I can't trace the root. Some people I know say there is no point hating when millions who have voted for them don't. They are legitimate representatives of the public. Isn't hating them better than hating the country and its people?'

'Why don't you hate the system instead as I had recommended in *Hind Swaraj*?'

'I know you had, but I can't make such fine distinctions when I feel so sick with these power-hungry monsters. They want to destroy everything I worked for . . . and what you achieved for us too.'

'They can't destroy the country . . . If they destroy it, where will they rule? They just want to change it according to their idea. You probably hate their idea more than you hate them. . .'

'I can't separate the two. Their idea drives them to be who they are—intolerant tricksters . . . They've come to power by lying at every step.'

'I must say you must think about this more carefully if you want to know what truth meant for me . . . and also why it had to be clubbed with non-violence. It sounds like a slogan, but it's not. It takes time to grasp. You can't do it in a hurry, especially when you feel so unhappy and desperate.'

My dialogue tapering off, I considered if the way Gandhi thought about truth was perhaps a bit too nebulous for people, both for his detractors and for his devotees. Things like 'tell me the truth' or 'don't tell me lies' are far from Gandhi's conception of truth. Those who doubted his motives may not have grasped his idea, but it worked like a spell on people who decided to follow his path to the end of their lives.

One such person was an English woman, Marjorie Sykes. I was lucky to see her a few times—first when she visited Kundeshwar and came to my school. K. and I had never seen an English woman before this, but we were both somewhat disappointed that this one wore *salwar kurta*, that too of khadi. She did look smart though with her sparkling white *dupatta* draped around her neck. Decades later when I saw her in Hoshangabad, she looked gaunt, but her clothes were just the same. I had taken time off some official work, so the meeting was short, but she gave me a signed copy of a small book she had written about Nai Talim or New Education—of the kind K. and I were enrolled in at Kundeshwar. I am sure she gave it because I reminded her of her visit to Kundeshwar and my basic school. On my way back from Hoshangabad, I glanced through the book, flipping through to the last page where she had described the abandoned experiment of Gandhian education. There, right at the very end, came these words: 'Inasmuch as it was a true idea, its time will come.' I took this sentence to be the pious sentiment of an English woman who had come to India to devote her life to Gandhi's commands. It was a nice, consoling thought to close a book with, that an idea that had died will one day return to life. Only recently, when I had begun to recover from the shock of the election results of Bhopal, a new, more plausible meaning of that sentence shot through my mind. Marjorie Sykes was referring to her faith that an idea born in the pursuit of goodness and truth does not die. Its time will come when the conditions are right.

It is somewhat like the idea that the Dalai Lama often invokes to explain the predicament of his people. It is a part of the Buddha's way. It is also a key idea in Jain faith to which Gandhi owed a number of his tenets: that everything—a stone, a speck of dust, not just a tree or a cat—is alive and enmeshed in a long series of circumstances and conditions. When a congenial combination gets a chance to be formed, what seemed dead comes alive, again. This is the kind of hope that drove Gandhi's politics of truth—that its day will come.

The historical Gandhi used 'truth' as a symbol—of an amalgam he was compounding throughout his life. The qualities or values blended into it were varied. Some of them were derived from tradition; others were derived from his legal practice, political experience and friendships. In the first category, we can recognize values like honesty and gratitude— to others who gave him something, and also to ancestors— and *santosh*—deceptively translatable as 'satisfaction'. In the old world to which this term belongs, it connotes the absence of greed. When there is no greed, it doesn't necessarily mean contentedness, which can suggest inertia resulting from physical and social comforts.

Then there is the second group of values and mental states in Gandhi's truth mixture. We can start the list with a thorough knowledge of all the facts. The others in this list might feel like quite a mouthful of the customary signs denoting political correctness and self-righteousness: justice, equality, rule of law and dignity of the individual, and, let me add, so on. The opening title in this list was unique to Gandhi: gathering facts with the help of common people, the wretched sufferers who attracted him right from when he started his legal practice in South Africa. Facts about their life and experience served as the truth that enabled Gandhi to translate his legal practice into politics. Faithfully recording what his hapless clients told him turned into a sophisticated non-violent weapon that Gandhi deftly held in his writing hand. Armed with trustworthy facts, he felt he could depend on the law of the land to press its rulers to deliver justice. They might do so reluctantly in the beginning and out of embarrassment, and with growing resentment. That very resentment would provide fuel for Gandhi's out-of-court politics.

Truth in his hand, and with no apparent axe of his own to grind, the young lawyer became a churner—of congealed muck. The churning released the kind of stench the European rulers of South Africa had never experienced in their history. And some of the stench crossed the ocean to reach India. As a 'coolie barrister', Gandhi hammered the banality out of clichés such as equality of all human beings, dignity and justice. He replicated in Champaran, a district of present-day northern Bihar, his strategy of collecting evidence of injustice directly from sufferers. Again, this time, his success in court translated into political victory. A personal theory of truth germinated. Having taken root, it never stopped growing in his fertile mind.

And he was religious. His statements like 'Truth is God' expressed the role that faith—unabashed religious belief— played in his life. Commentators try to separate the faith from his insightful politics. The attempt to make Gandhi fit into the conventional frame of secularism continues with greater urgency now, when the insidious politics of religion has gained dominance and that too through democratic procedures. The astute engineers of such politics now seem to be comfortably placed. Their much-vaunted religious faith has nothing to do with Gandhi's religiosity. His 'gift of the fight', as Marjorie Sykes termed it (in the title of a book she wrote with Jahangir Patel), was inspired by spiritual goals and not by narrow ritualistic dogma, banal as a chant. Gandhi's faith demanded personal integrity. Without it, despair would have finished off the fight prematurely or altered its character. Faced with the persistent indifference of authority and police brutality, anyone other than Gandhi would have changed track or given up.

I am also battling despair and the anxiety that the new political ethos will soon consume my beloved country. I know the State. I served it. Official violence and licence to hate are beyond its capacity to handle. It terrifies me to imagine what will happen if the State crumbles. When I read Gandhi, I feel lighter. I feel glad that someone so strong and important had imagined my pain. I sense his touch and it heals me, for some time. I decide to stay away from TV debates and rabid newscasters. For a day or two I am fine, then my terror returns.

It is easier to borrow some hope from Gandhi's way than to work up hope by yourself these days. The political system is negotiating a curve where India, so arduously assembled, can get badly damaged and be lost for a long, long time, perhaps for ever. The old question, for people like me are outdated, has returned to haunt us: 'Who are we?' When the whole world appears to be obsessed with identity, how can we escape it? The clash between competitive nationalist identities that resulted in two awful worldwide wars of the twentieth century has not died down. India need not have been infected by this competitive turmoil, but we surrendered, and now the pathogen has taken a virulent form.

For Gandhi, the search for truth also meant getting to the bottom of things. These days, official narrative is put out, alongside a formal inquiry, to create public confidence.

What if the bottom is already known or has become common knowledge—so common that no one in the public cares anymore? After every mess, an investigation is initiated. The public knows and believes that what it knows is the truth. But the government persists with its narrative. It goes on and on with finding the truth. The ludicrous American President Donald Trump was in Delhi when arson and killings started in the north-eastern part of the city. No one was embarrassed. The local government of Delhi felt protected from any blame for the riots and how the police behaved. The police are under the Union government. They were not embarrassed or even anxious. They knew their job would start after a few days of killings and burning of properties. Dutifully, they registered cases against student leaders, teachers and so on—those who had nothing to do with the riots. The police, I am sure, knew that these citizens were not the kind who shoot or stab. When a university teacher asked, during his questioning at a police station why a local politician was not arrested despite his slogan, which asked people to shoot and kill, having been filmed, the investigating officer told the teacher: 'That was a joke.'

And that is what the pursuit of truth often is these days. It runs into thousands of pages. The judges who supposedly read these pages do not tell the prosecution that the inquiry was a farce. They stick to the convention that requires the maintenance of good faith in the police force. If someone tried writing a crime novel about the riots, he would soon give up, for there would be no room for suspense or revelation. The odour of truth can't be fictionalized. It is so real and omnipresent that even the ridiculous Trump and his wife must have smelt it. She was visiting a school in South Delhi when smoke was rising on the eastern horizon. She sat in a class where the 'happiness curriculum' of the Delhi government was being taught.

One recent mutation of truth-seeking is the Right to Information. It's known as 'RTI'. People can now demand a copy of an officer's file noting by exercising this new right. As an officer serving the government at one of its highest rungs, I knew how frustrating the State's opacity could be for ordinary people. When Aruna Roy started her campaign for the Right to Information, it looked like the beginning of a revolution. She herself had been an IAS officer, so she knew how radical a difference this right would make to relations between the State and the citizen. At the start of Roy's campaign, the prospects of this right being encoded into law looked bleak. But then, lo and behold, it happened. Everything appeared so easy and truth so close by. For just ten rupees, you could compel a majestic ministry to reveal its inner workings, even a confidential noting. Like so much else happening in that unexpected spring of the early Manmohan Singh era, it was hard to resist the thought that India was marching with a new resolve towards becoming a true democracy.

Who didn't enjoy the illusion that from now onwards, well-guarded power would feel compelled to practice transparency. For a short while, the new Right to Information offered the hope that officers and ministers would become accountable. But it did not take long for the old reflexes to return. Minions of the powerful started tracking the citizen who had sent the query. Digital technology, especially the bio-metric identity given to each citizen, enhanced the State's reach and power. The ordinary citizen eventually withdrew and RTI became a new site of activism—professional file-diggers. The officer in charge of handling RTI questions could distinguish professionals from genuine applicants, whose numbers declined rapidly. Some of them were found dead. The splendour of RTI as an instrument of truth diminished as fast as it had grown.

The idea of giving a biometric identity to every man, woman and child was hailed as a breakthrough in governance. It would cure India of corruption, the needy alone would reap State benefits, and so on went the chatter; and it got louder when they enforced the linking of the unique twelve-digit identity number to phone and bank account. Digital companies and the State are now firmly embraced allies: one shapes and serves citizens' needs, the other keeps them in a tight grip. But 'Digital India' is a lot more than that. It has integrated India thoroughly enough to endure any amount of ideological consolidation around the vision of religious separatism. Those who hold State power can now hound whomever they choose. The spirit of dissent, germinated after a long struggle, has been subdued by the digitally equipped State. Exemplar dissenters can rot in jail on charges that can neither be proved nor disproved as trials need not start for years and will take many more years to conclude.

A new era has set in. Things have become so transparent that the exercise of RTI became redundant. The grand old machinery of the State became adept at taking decisions in ways that could cheerfully survive a silly RTI activist's query. And this was just the first step. The State apparatus soon fell into the hands of people who were used to living in a secret community, a brotherhood of malcontents. They were committed to their distant goals, carefully flagged under vows of good, open conduct in the short run. In their list of values, a blank space replaced truth. Their truth was far too momentous to be revealed to anyone outside the sworn-in fraternity. It had honed its skill of guarding the truth for a hundred years. One of the skills it had mastered to perfection was mendacity. With its help, they shed consistency. After a meeting with their guru, Gandhi had said: 'It was impossible to rely upon their word. They appear to be highly reasonable when talked to, but they had no compunction in acting in exact contradiction to what they said.'

Laborious probing of a doubt is important for sustaining hope, but when probing becomes irrelevant, hope dies, and the doubt nibbles at your concern. Why bother, you ask, and you hear the others, who are better adjusted, say, don't.

A few months after Munna's death, there was a rape and murder in a village in Uttar Pradesh. The girl belonged to a Dalit family. She had been brutally attacked near her home and died in a Delhi hospital. The case had become so charged because of media frenzy by then that the police and district authorities thought it best to quickly cremate her body before any medical or forensic examination could be carried out. It might have proved to the satisfaction of judges that she was raped before being strangled. The remarkable opacity thus achieved made the State fearless about any legal consequences that might have been incurred. A Kerala journalist who tried to visit the village was arrested under a law that does not permit a judge to grant bail. No one could travel to Hathras during that week although the town is on a newly built highway. It separates the village where the girl had lived from the primary school from which she had dropped out a decade earlier when the highway was built. The heavy traffic on the route had made it perilous for children to walk across to

school. When the highway was being built,
a digital register of all schools in the
country had been created to improve the
State machinery's transparency. Data about
the murdered girl's primary school can be
seen on the Internet. These data show that
it had a separate toilet for girls. And a
ramp for disabled children.

Truth had already become science when K. and I were young. At
school, they started teaching science as the ultimate truth soon
after Independence. The IAS officers of my generation knew, but
we were also told in our induction training that although India's
financial resources were limited, it could not afford to neglect any
sector of science, no matter how expensive it was—from high-
yielding crops to nuclear and space sciences. The last two were
crucial for national security just as big dams and giant steel plants
were crucial for prosperity as Nehru had said. Although he had
become an icon of scientific temper, it wasn't quite clear what
it meant to have such a temper. At my secondary school, I got
somewhat confused about this matter one day.

It was the grade XI physics practical class. Scindia school
was well endowed, and it had some remarkable teachers. One
of them, Mr Rastogi, was well known for his erudition and
creative ways of explaining abstractions to distracted boys. He
was tall, well-built, with an impressive silver moustache. With
no wrinkle on his forehead, he looked young; on days when he
wore a yellow checked T-shirt, he looked like he was one of
us. He never scolded but argued with force in his voice. That
day, he was arguing with my deskmate Narayan Bannerjee. We
had just completed the practical lesson for finding the refractive
index of a prism. Narayan's answer was accurate to the third
number after the decimal.

'How did you get this so accurate?' Mr Rastogi asked.

'I was careful, sir,' replied Narayan.

'That's good, but is it possible to be so accurate?'

'Why not, sir?'

'Because no prism is perfect . . .'

'What do you mean, sir?'

'I mean you can't get a perfect reading . . . unless you cheat.'

Narayan's face fell. Perhaps Mr Rastogi realized that he had hurt Narayan unnecessarily. He explained why no experiment in science can be done perfectly, no matter how experienced the person performing it is. Even a simple fact like the boiling point of water was an average because the actual figure depends on the quality of the water and on the measuring device. Everyone in the class was stunned to hear all this. We had been under the impression that science was all about facts and they were all crisp and unchangeable. To our young minds, Mr Rastogi's wisdom came across like a contradiction of Nehru's faith in scientific temper. Mr Rastogi's last words to Narayan that day were: 'When you get older and study more science, you will realize that scientific knowledge is always evolving.'

The opposite happened. When I did get older, I came to see that in modern times, science had monopoly over truth. It may not offer finality, but in general it was a good idea to prefer science over other sources. In matters like disease and medicine, and natural phenomena like eclipses and earthquakes, there was no point in clinging to old ideas. Then, stealthily, the lack of faith in science became associated with illiteracy. That's how the poor think: they worship a village deity instead of going to a doctor, explained a guest speaker at the administrative academy. He was an eminent sociologist. His message was simple: modernity can't coexist with superstition: it must be eradicated, like a disease. What about God? No one dared ask him. Nor did I. It seemed silly to ask such a question although

a glass frame in my primary school had never slipped from
my memory. It said, 'God is truth', and below it was printed
the name of the person, in smaller letters, who had made this
utterance: Mahatma Gandhi.

Later in life, Gandhi reversed it and said, 'Truth is God'.
By the time of this playful reversal, he had experienced the
problem of communicating faith. I suppose he knew that
some people found it irritating when he attributed his political
decisions to God's command. These people were rationally
minded non-believers who wanted science, not God, to guide
humanity. Gandhi's insistence that God alone was the truth,
was probably a bit exaggerated. The reverse—'Truth is God'—
looks more reasonable. It doesn't make an a priori demand
for belief in God and opens the way for non-believers to join
in. The reversal—of his own earlier phrase—also suggests an
ongoing experiment, with himself, his search. It makes him a
scientist of a sort.

My present state of mind impels me to find traces of
Gandhi in strange places. He seems woven into my life in many
ways. Or maybe, it's because I need him so much that I notice
things that help me understand him better. I am not talking
about relics; the new masters can create and sell them to the
tourist. No, I am talking about traces that I don't need to find—
because the traces find me. In a recent novel by the Irish writer
Colm Tóibín, I came across a dialogue between a struggling,
sad mother and an incommunicative son. He was explaining
what it means to believe in God. I saw in it a remarkable
exegesis of Gandhi's faith, and the difficulty he continues to
have convincing the secular-minded that God exists. The novel
Nora Webster tells the story of an Irish widow's struggle after her
husband's death. She brings up her four children with courage,
fighting her own grief in her struggle to live. Her third child,
Donal, is a taciturn, moody teenager, and he stammers. After

reading this conversation between Donal and his mother, I felt I knew Gandhi's God:

'D-do you know about the p-paradox of f-faith?' he asked her when he was finished eating.

'I'm not sure I do,' she said.

'Father Moorehouse gave us a sermon on it. J-just a s-small g-group who are doing s-special re-re-religious st-studies.'

'What is it?' she asked.

'In order to b-believe, you have to b-believe,' he said. 'Once you have faith, then you can b-believe more, but you c-can't believe until you b-begin to b-believe. That f-first b-belief is a mystery. It is like a g-gift. And then the r-rest is r-rational, or it c-can be.'

'But it can't be proved,' she said. 'You can only sense it.'

'Yes, b-but he says it's not like p-proof. It's n-not adding two and two, but more like adding light to w-water.'

'That sounds very deep.'

'No, it's simple really. It explains things.'

She noticed that he had not stammered on the last sentence.

'You must have s-something first,' he went on. 'I suppose th-that is what he is saying.'

'And if you don't?'

'That is the atheist position.'*

Donal's logic applies rather nicely to Gandhi, especially to his earnest sense of make-belief—that he was a resident of the kingdom of God. The idea of God he alluded to on different occasions helps us imagine the kingdom that God might govern. Gandhi's indebtedness to Leo Tolstoy and his book, *The Kingdom of God Is Within You*, is well known. He was criticized for it as well as for showing so much devotion

---

* From *Nora Webster*, a novel by Colm Toibin, published by Viking, 2014.

to Christianity. Gandhi carved out his own interpretation of religiosity without weakening his rootedness in several traditional ideas, symbols and literary sources associated with Hinduism. In his ethical code, one can read several different and occasionally divergent elements. Some can be seen as his inheritance from his mother and the local ethos of Kathiawar. A temple where his mother sometimes visited had no deity and an inscription from the Koran was etched on the entrance along with a verse from the Gita. A strong element of Jain beliefs also shaped his religious socialization when he was young.

Gandhi used the word 'truth' to convey a larger meaning. His autobiography, published in weekly instalments in the late 1920s, when he was himself in his late fifties, gives us a clue to his early encounters with the word. The subtitle he gave to the story of his life also offers a glimpse of the accommodative meaning that 'truth' had acquired for him. His *experiments with truth* could hardly be all about truth in the common sense of fidelity to facts. Early in his autobiography, he recalls his anxiety to overcome 'doubts' about matters of religious faith. He records how reading the story of creation given in the Manusmriti, made him 'incline somewhat towards atheism'.[*] He also recalls asking an elder cousin his doubts, but he too did not help; instead, he said that 'these questions ought not to be raised at your age, that they will get resolved with age.' 'But one thing,' Gandhi says, 'took deep root in me—the conviction that morality is the basis of things, and that truth is the substance of all morality. Truth became my sole objective. It began to grow in magnitude every day, and my definition of it also has been ever widening.' No clearer statement is required to recognize that Gandhi treated truth as a symbol—of the ideals he saw as ingredients of morality.

---

[*] M.K. Gandhi's *An Autobiography* published by Penguin Books with Introduction and Notes by Tridip Suhrud, 2018, p. 98.

There was a deeper struggle underneath this approach. Chapter X of the autobiography records his self-recrimination over his lustful start to married life as an adolescent. The tone is confessional though it is hard to imagine that at this point in his life he had already absorbed the guilt-ridden devotion associated with Christianity. His memory of reading aloud Tulsidas's Ramayana to his ailing father doesn't quite prepare us for his devotion to Tulsidas and Lord Rama. An old family nurse told him to chant 'Ramanama' to overcome his fear of ghosts and spirits. Gandhi's account of his upbringing indicates that the edifice of his later religious life was firmly established early. Belief in the *varna* system was an essential part of it. Gandhi never forbore expressing his faith in this system. It took him a long time to overcome his early induction in this matter. His own experience with the lower castes and Ambedkar's strident movement nudged Gandhi towards realizing, towards the final phase of his life and career, that Varnashrama Dharma—the dharma based on the varna division—was not a moral idea. Its positive imprinting on young Gandhi's mind must have derived strength from Tulsidas's Ramayana: its prosody, its musicality, and its vast, compelling canvas.

In his rendering of the Ramayana, better known as the Ramcharitmanas, Tulsidas has given the masses a text they need no one's help or literacy to decipher. A voluminous book, it needs time, sustained over months, to read. It is a lot easier to sing, and that is what happens in thousands of villages of the Vindhya–Gangetic plains. It forms a background text for the Ramlila performance during the month of Karthik, leading to the festival of Diwali. As a young boy, I craved the opportunity to sit with the poorer folk of our royal neighbourhood, to sing like the other children assembled inside and outside a Shiva temple. My father was clear: his son could not be allowed to sit with a sweating huddle inside a temple that had no window

whatsoever, just a door that was nearly blocked by the crowd
sitting and singing inside. Yet, despite these restrictions,
I managed to pick up a smattering of acquaintance with
Tulsidas's celebrated text. My secret induction into it was
assiduously managed by Tijia, one of our maidservants. I will
return to her life later, in a different context, but for now her
memory as the affectionate tutor who trained me to recite
verses from the Ramcharitmanas will suffice. I especially liked
the portions about the tormenting words Kaikeyi spoke to her
husband, the old king Dashratha and the commotion in the
palace that followed. Then there were sections of Rama's life
in the forest that I enjoyed reciting. The description of his
final battle was somewhat confusing. A small boy could hardly
make sense of this allegorical picture of Rama standing barefoot
facing the demon-king astride a chariot with all kinds of lethal
weapons. Tulsidas's listing of Lord Rama's moral qualities, in
a self-narration format, made little sense to me in the context
of a fierce battle about to start. It must have greatly appealed
to Gandhi. It contains a comprehensive statement of Gandhi's
Truth. I am going to quote it here from the English translation
by F.S. Growse.* Without the music of Tulsidas's words and
rhythm, the passage sounds a bit tedious.

When Vibhisana beheld Ravana on a chariot and Rama on
foot, he became apprehensive: his extreme affection made him
doubtful of mind, and falling at his feet, he cried tenderly: 'My
Lord, you have neither a chariot nor shoes to your feet, how can
you conquer so powerful a warrior?'

'Harden, my friend,' replied the Lord of Grace, 'A conqueror
has a different kind of chariot. Manliness and courage are
his chariot wheels; unflinching truthfulness and morality his

---

* *The Ramayana of Tulsidasa* by F.S. Growse, published by Motilal
Banarsidas, Delhi, First revised edition, 1978, pp. 586–587.

banners and standards; strength, discretion, self-control and benevolence his horses, with grace, mercy and equanimity for their harness; prayer to Mahadeva his unerring charioteer; continence his shield, contentment his sword, alms-giving his axe, knowledge his mighty spear, and perfect science his stout bow. His pure and constant soul stands for a quiver, his pious practices of devotion for a sheaf of arrows, and the revenue he pays to Brahmanas and his gurus is his impenetrable coat of mail. There is no equipment for victory compared to this, nor is there any enemy, my friend, who can conquer the man who rides upon this chariot of righteousness.'

'He who owns such a powerful chariot as this is a hero who can vanquish even that great and terrible enemy, the world; harken, friend, and fear not.'

Gandhi's fusion of religious sources of inspiration was adventurous from the start. One finds no hint of hesitation on his part in drawing so much from Christianity while maintaining his firm Vaishnava Dharma. Between the Gita, the Ramayana and the Bible, he seems to have no preference. Although Tagore also proposed a religion of his own, Manava Dharma or the Religion of Man, Gandhi's faith was a bolder mix. Readings from the Gita, the Ramayana and the Bhakti poets shaped both his private and public self. And then there is a sharp Christian streak. By the time he became India's most audible voice, his contemporaries were becoming uneasy. For example, in a 1926 conversation, Sri Aurobindo says that Gandhi 'is largely influenced by Tolstoy, the Bible and has a strong Jain tinge in his teachings; at any rate more than by the Indian scriptures - the Upanishads or the Gita, which he interprets in the light of his own idea'. Gandhi perceived the celebrated dialogue between the nervous warrior Arjuna and Lord Krishna as a metaphor, a conflict of ideas raging in Arjuna's mind.

Given India's circumstances today, it might seem that Gandhi's influence on Hinduism will not last. Only time will tell. The greatest alteration he attempted to bring in Hinduism was to incorporate a sense of collective guilt which, in Christianity, is recognized as a basic value. Gandhi must have noticed its absence in Hinduism. To feel guilty can have contradictory implications, in that a sense of permanent guilt can create despair as well as inspiration. By making the cross a key symbol of Christ's sacrifice for the sake of humanity, Christianity attempts to impel us towards aspiring to be good, not letting Christ's sacrifice go waste. Gandhi's assassination arouses similar thoughts, but the association of guilt with inspiration goes deeper. Gandhi invokes the feeling many Bhakti poets have expressed in their devotional compositions: utter humility in the imagined presence of the divine. Surdas and Tulsidas use self-derision as a preface to awakening into a new realization of their hope that the divine will give them shelter. In this poetic tradition, guilt was already a part of the Indian moral tradition, but the idea of collective guilt for things that the evil-minded have done is brought into play by Gandhi.

Gandhi gave us a reformed and enriched version of Hinduism, and by doing so, he inspired millions like me to develop personal ways of sustaining faith in God. Was this a secular creed for a modernizing society? That no longer seems to be the case although secularism, as a marker of personality, strongly tempts us to enlist Gandhi. One hardly need say that his India will have to be secular, but that does not say much, especially about his faith and the importance of being a believer. Gandhi's worldview is not fully comprehensible without appreciating the importance of God in it. His rationality is embedded in faith and religiosity. Declaring him a liberal whose thought and practices are rooted in reason is to miss a source that gave him vitality throughout life. I suppose the problem is with us, with our inability to accept God's existence after scientists, as a professional community, have declared God unsustainable. They have persuaded us, and with the help of political leaders, compelled us, to believe that there is no object or occurrence to explain in which God's presence or role is required.

The Kingdom of God is a place where nothing is not within the ruler's sight; no misdeed or evil thought is hidden to him. He sees all and cares for all too. In such a kingdom, the practice of any value cannot be worthwhile if it is merely personal. Giving it value would mean making it everybody's value. Thus, if Gandhi was looking for freedom, he knew he would not attain it without making it everyone's quest. What all would freedom cover? Fear, for sure, to begin with.

'Truth is God' conveys two joined ideas. The first is that the pursuit of truth is like looking for God. Linked to it is the second idea: that the search—for both truth and God—is a personal pursuit, so you need not worry if the search doesn't impress others. If they feel it lacks authenticity, so be it. People can hold different truths if the truths help them maintain faith in their journey. If this indeed was Gandhi's view, it was not far from the Jain philosophy of *anekant*, which roughly translates as 'diverse ends'. It has an additional echo which reveals itself if you play with the term. If you break it differently, you will think it means 'non-loneliness'. It suggests that if we are all pursuing our own different truths, we share a common search, hence none of us needs to feel alone. One thing we know for sure about Gandhi is that he never felt lonely. Historians may not agree. They like to think that at the end of his life, when the Partition looked inevitable, he felt abandoned by his intimate associates.

That he decided that 'Truth Is God' does not mean he abandoned his earlier position where 'God was Truth', the only truth and not an imaginary being. So, if science denied God and made people suspect the existence of God, then one could not believe in both science and God. Between God and science, Gandhi would have any day preferred to suspect science. He came into conflict with Tagore on what causes earthquakes. Tagore had great respect for Gandhi, but on this matter, Tagore was somewhat outraged. He wrote to Gandhi that he should not propagate an idea that had no basis. Gandhi maintained his position. The exchange of letters between the two men ended in a stalemate. But if Gandhi had tried, he might have won the debate by asking Tagore a simple, rather scientific question: 'How can you prove that earthquakes are not caused by God to express his indignation?'

Truth telling is often associated with a harsh candour. That does not bother the truthful, but that cannot be true of Gandhi. He was not inclined to be rude to anyone—for not agreeing. Regarding seismology, Tagore did not merely disagree with Gandhi; he accused Gandhi of not adhering to his highest principle—the truth—in this matter. Tagore rightly assumed that like any other educated person, Gandhi would know that God had little to do with an earthquake, especially with the choice of place where it causes its devastating effect. On the grounds of this assumption, Tagore felt that Gandhi was not being sincere in arguing that Bihar was targeted with a terrible earthquake in 1934 *because* the practice of untouchability was so rampant there. Tagore didn't say that Gandhi was teaching falsehoods, but there was a hint at that motive. In his reply, Gandhi elaborated on his view that nature too is governed by, and therefore is an expression of, a higher moral truth in which the practice of untouchability cannot be accommodated.

Belief in a punitive God whose wrath can mercilessly kill and injure thousands in a few seconds does not sit well with our image of Gandhi as a meek and mild devotee, but this idea of God is not freakish in the least. Gandhi's religious faith

extended to all major traditions. Not just the Old Testament
and the Koran uphold belief in, and fear of, God's fury, but
within Hinduism too there are ample instances and stories
wherein divine anger is acknowledged. Gandhi's argument
about why a bad earthquake struck Bihar may seem like an
affectation from a scientific position, and Tagore takes that
view. The difference between them arose because Gandhi's
view of truth was wider than that which science demands:
respect for evidence. Gandhi's problem with science arises from
its negation of a higher authority—a judge whose voice is hard
to hear if you're occupied with your own goals.

Moral correctness was not what Gandhi was after.
One can find many instances of moral incorrectness in his
decisions and actions. It all depends on the reference point.
In his case, the reference point was the tension between
truth and violence. The younger Gandhi did commit some
acts of violence in the name of truth—his truth. Instances
of roughness, for example, in the way he treated his wife,
are evidence that at the start, Gandhi could react like any
impulsive, rather typical husband. The later Gandhi tuned
his search for truth to the harder demands of non-violence
in an increasingly aggressive ethos. The historical Gandhi
stands somewhere between these two extremes, but closer
to his second cornerstone, as he recognized that the lure of
violence was far greater than the lure of untruth. Violence
attracts men, he must have thought, because it offers the
promise of peace after a short, bloody embrace.

Munna called me up early one morning in
January and asked in an agitated voice,
'Did you read that the Sabarmati Ashram is
going to have a facelift?'
    'Facelift? For what?' I said.

'They want to make it attractive for tourists.'

'But it already attracts a lot of tourists.'

'No, no . . . It'll be on a different scale now . . . It will be a fun place—like what the gallery at Gandhi Smriti has become.'

I recalled going there with Munna some time back. Gandhi Smriti (the place where Gandhi was murdered) looked familiar, but the upstairs exhibition in the main building of Birla House had been transformed into a press-button-fun space for children. Luckily, the spot where Gandhi was assassinated, and the lawn around had not been touched—yet.

'They have some awful ideas about what Sabarmati Ashram must look like . . . The riverfront has gone into cement. The report I read last night says they were inspired by Shanghai.'

I didn't know how to respond. So, I asked, 'Did you walk this morning? It was so chilly—and cloudy . . .'

'No, I didn't . . . I didn't sleep well.' Then, after a pause, Munna said, 'I am going back to sleep.'

'Oh, that's good,' I said. 'I'm glad you called . . . otherwise I might still be . . .'

He interrupted. 'I'm sorry I woke you up . . . I guess I was so upset I didn't think.'

Gandhi's last words invoked Lord Rama, but Lord Krishna's weapon-less leadership in the famous battle of Kurukshetra in the Mahabharata must have attracted him more. It was Tagore who mentioned Lord Krishna while admiring Gandhi's ability to mobilize people. Tagore's reference was cautionary; he wrote to Gandhi that his influence on the common masses would not serve in the long run. When the non-cooperation movement was at its peak, Gandhi had suddenly withdrawn it and the people had heeded his bidding that they stop and return home. 'When you are not around,' Tagore asked, 'who would tell the people to go back?' Tagore was alluding to Lord Krishna's flute that had a mesmerizing effect on the young: they rushed out of their homes to listen to the melody and, went back when the music ended.

I can't imagine how Gandhi viewed being compared to Lord Krishna. He must have felt embarrassed, inspired as he was by the real Krishna's preaching to Arjuna with whom he identified later in life. Gandhi remained immensely modest throughout his life, and also open and energetic like a child, excited to meet anyone and enjoy whatever came his way. He knew how deep the tendency to deify was set in the Indian mind. Yet, it must have been hard for a man just about fifty to learn that he was like Lord Krishna. He must have taken it in his stride, I suppose, or perhaps his fate—to be accepted like a dress people wanted him to don. Historians say Gandhi chose the mendicant-like attire that became his permanent political image. They must be wrong, and R.K. Narayan must be right, in how he starts his novel, *The Guide*. It is *not* crafted like an allegory, but its framing evokes Gandhi. A man comes out of prison after spending many long years inside. He doesn't know where to go. Tired and hungry, he lies under a tree where he is noticed by a villager. He throws a cloth over the sleeping man who he thinks must be a wandering holy man. And when

the man awakes, he finds himself bound into the villagers'
perception of him as a holy man. This is where Narayan starts
his story, which ends with the man invoking the rain God
because the villagers believe he possesses magical powers. And
then, someone says it actually is raining in the nearby hills.
That is where the story ends.

When he returned to India from South Africa, Gandhi
was only in his late forties. He found himself imprisoned in
people's expectations of him and in their faith that he alone
could fulfil these impossible-looking hopes. Such was his
reputation already, in a land that he hardly knew, beyond
the vague sense of loyalty that an educated man might have,
returning after a very long gap to his enslaved country. He had
to prepare himself for a life he could hardly escape, daunting
though it must have looked. His own guide, Gokhale, too
died soon, leaving him to be led onwards by his own intuition
and sense of things. The battle waiting for him to join was
no less vast and fierce than the Mahabharata. For a poet, that
too a mystic like Tagore, to recognize Gandhi's influence by
invoking Lord Krishna was one thing, but the comparison
became more palpable when a politician junior to him in
age, Rajagopalachari, assigned him the role of the charioteer
in India's epic battle. How could he possibly disappoint such
tall and venerated men? And there was his own devout mind,
full of doubt about every reward and pleasure that the modern
world was promising to mankind in return for the loss of faith
in anything higher than science and logic.

The comparison with Lord Krishna had entered the
popular imagination by the late 1920s. A Hindi jingle from that
period compares Gandhi's *charkha* with Lord Krishna's flute.
K.'s mother told me that she used to recite this jingle when she
was eleven, the year she lost her father. A Punjabi activist from
the late 1920s, Gaura Devi, had organized picketing of shops

selling liquor and Manchester-cotton textile. K.'s mother was part of Gaura Devi's girls' brigade. Gandhi had never been to her town, but his image as an incarnation of Lord Krishna had spread. The only lines stuck in the young girl's memory of that jingle went like this:

Ve bansi khoob bajaate the,
Ye charkha khoob chalaate hein.

He—Lord Krishna—used to play on his flute;
he (Gandhi) spins on his charkha.

As Gandhi grew older and found himself pitted against circumstances that he was unable to influence, he must have found comfort in the Gita. His call for Quit India received a resounding public response, but the commotion led to turmoil in many places. State suppression and public outrage both turned violent. How disturbed Gandhi was by the widespread public disorder is hard to say. Two decades earlier, just one report of violence in a village of Uttar Pradesh had sufficed to convince Gandhi that the movement had gone wrong. Now, he seemed more tolerant or perhaps somewhat resigned—not in the sense that he did not care; rather, in the sense of having attained a higher perspective that releases a warrior from seeking the outcome of his effort in his own terms. Francis Hutchins was right in interpreting Quit India as a call of a driven man. This was not the first time that Gandhi had attributed his decision to the command of a higher power. Unfortunately, a hard secular view cannot concede the role of divine inspiration in shaping Gandhi's political decisions. His public avowal of being guided by divine authority made him seem an eccentric figure. Many found this an example of odious self-righteousness. Such people will laugh at me for saying that Gandhi helped me recover from my shock and depression. I suppose a totally secular person or someone who denies the existence of higher powers cannot accept Gandhi's claim to be guided by God or the strength he has given me.

Gandhi probably visualized a dramatic final sacrifice and expected it as his Karma. That it would work—to calm down hateful passions and establish peace—was also part of his faith and a metaphorical translation of the title of a crucial chapter in the Mahabharata: 'Antim Prayatna' or 'Final Effort'. Lord Krishna did not succeed in his final effort to achieve peace. Gandhi's *antim prayatna* did. Leaving himself open to be assassinated—by a man whose guides had honed his resolve to eliminate Gandhi—was the final instance of Gandhi's playful experimentation with truth. Psychoanalyst Eric Erikson is right to draw attention to the determined playfulness of Gandhi as a small boy—nicknamed Munia—in order to make sense of *Gandhi's Truth*. Erikson uses this insight to explain several episodes in Gandhi's pathway through an unusual life.

Three days before Gandhi was assassinated, in an interview the American journalist Vincent Sheean said to Gandhi: 'What I wish to ask is this: how can a righteous battle produce a catastrophic result?' Gandhi's reply was that 'if violent means are used, there will be a bad result'. Apparently, Gandhi was referring to the violence that had taken place in the final phase of the freedom struggle, under the Quit India movement and since then. 'As I read the Gita, even the first chapter, the battlefield of Kurukshetra is in the heart of man. I must tell you that orthodox scholars have criticized my interpretation of the Gita as being unduly influenced by the Sermon on the Mount.' Moments later, Sheean recalls, Gandhi added: 'There is one more learned book in existence which supports my interpretation of the Gita. But even if there were no such book, and even if it could be proved that my interpretation was wrong, I would still believe it.' It is hard to say which 'learned book' Gandhi was referring to. A day later when Sheean met Gandhi again, he read out to him the opening verse of the Isha Upanishad, translating it from the Sanskrit original: 'the whole world is the garment of the Lord. Renounce it, then, and receive it back as the gift of God.' Sheean had fixed another meeting with Gandhi a few days later, but it was not to be. His memoir of the two conversations he had that week shows that Gandhi was ready to make a final sacrifice for his cause, aware as he was that the cause had failed.

In that final phase of Gandhi's struggle to achieve India's freedom, awful things were happening all over. Hate had ousted amity and tolerance. The historians who have commented on Gandhi's isolation have overlooked the spiritual strategy he might have been contemplating. His assassination revealed it. In submitting his life peacefully and voluntarily to the assassin, he performed an act of passive defiance—overcoming the universal human instinct to save oneself. With this move, Gandhi achieved instant peace in the vast sub-continent's agitated mind. It silenced his arch-enemies for a long, long time. Clarity and good sense, that had evaporated from the ethos, returned, snuffing out the hate and the strife Partition had unleashed. Nathuram Godse's pistol enabled Gandhi to restore peace. It was yet another synonym for Gandhi's truth. The shock transformation of chaos into peace enabled Nehru—Gandhi's chosen successor—to join hands afresh with Patel, consolidate the new republic and stay in power long enough—seventeen years—to create a sense of direction in an injured nation. I wouldn't have guessed, even after becoming an adult, how wounded India was at the time of its birth if I had not been so close to K. in my childhood.

I came to know many years after leaving home that his parents had been devastated by Partition. During one of my vacation visits, K.'s mother asked me about my new school. The

story of India's independence had been enacted as a play that
summer, before the start of the vacation. I told aunty about
the play and how it ended, with a brief reference to Partition.
Something opened up and she suddenly started to talk about her
life after Partition. She told me what it meant to cross the Atari
border a day after Partition. K.'s father, she said, went back
to Lahore to retrieve his law books. When he did not return,
everyone in their family thought he had been killed. No one in
my family knew or could have imagined what had happened to
K.'s family. Nor did K.. His mother and father had maintained
total silence about their past. It felt strange to know more than
he did about his parents.

That was not all. My conversations with K.'s mother
continued over my later visits home. In one of these, she told
me what she had learnt from her brother about Gandhi's death.
Her narration of his memory of the evening of Gandhi's murder
became a vivid reality for me. Thousands of people had walked
to Birla House where Gandhi's body lay. They wept when they
heard Nehru choking as he talked of Gandhi in the light of
a gas lantern at the gate of Birla House. Everything changed
that evening. People felt as if they had made a terrible mistake.
They cried and repented. The city and the country were saved
from further self-destruction. Such was the effect of Gandhi's
violent end.

In my tormented mind, Munna, the nickname that K.'s
mother had given me has continued to remind me of her deep
affection for me. I can recall so many occasions of my boyhood
when K. sensed it and felt jealous. He always felt his mother
had no time for him because she was so busy with her school
and social welfare work throughout the district. My memory
is so sharply different. My mother hardly knew how to express
love. As a princess, she was used to avoiding any emotional

expression in front of others, and there was no room for
seclusion in our mansion.

K. and I lost our mothers a long time ago. The name K.'s
mother had given me out of love seems, at times, to have changed
its meaning for me. I feel so low these days that I can't control
my mind when it alters the past, denigrating its happiness and
glory, even the love I received in plenty. In my darker moments,
I begin to think that K.'s mother called me Munna because she
had fathomed my deep timidity, so markedly contrasting with
my father's he-man personality. Despite her great affection and
my gratitude, when I'm in this state, I can't stop suspicion from
invading my disturbed mind. When this strain takes over, I feel
ashamed of my nickname because it matches my present life
in retirement: brooding, helpless, withdrawn. I have 'become'
a Munna; someone hardly meriting a Bundela warrior caste
name like Viresh Pratap Singh.

It is clear there is nothing I can do about anything. Probably
many others feel like me, but my state of mind surprises me.
That's not the way I have ever been—not as a child, not as
a teenager, never in my married life or my career. Something
so radical has occurred that I don't recognize myself anymore.
I eel drained of hope, and incapable of expressing my outrage.
I have lost faith in institutions that I had respected and worked
for. I am so dejected and at the same time mad that if someone
asks me to explain what it is that makes me feel so angry, I am
not sure I will be able to explain it coherently. There is a private
sense of failure as well: I need no one to convince me that I have
failed my father. I was proud of him because he was fearless. I
hear his voice saying I am an unworthy son because I feel so
weak and debilitated. How can I not? A famous historian has
said that India will take fifty years to rebuild itself. People who
are in their active phase of life agree that nothing much can be

done about the destruction we see around us—of institutions, standards, values and a lot more. Many senior civil servants have turned around, dropping their secular faith like old pants with turned-up cuffs. Why should they lose what opportunities the regime offers, they ask. If I were in my fifties, perhaps I too would have felt and behaved like them?

The psychologist Ashis Nandy has rightly said in one of his interviews on present-day politics that we *are* in big trouble. As a nation, we have been thrown off course, pushed far down from where Gandhi had brought us. His own fantasy was loftier, and some feel pleased that he didn't live to push India any further. Gokhale, whom Gandhi regarded as his guru, had laughed when he read *Hind Swaraj*—the book in which Gandhi's vision of freedom and happiness for India is best described. In his autobiography, Gandhi recalls Gokhale saying to him: 'After you have stayed a year in India, your views will correct themselves.'* I must confess that I had, till quite recently, only seen and remembered *Hind Swaraj* through Nehruvian eyes. In fact, I found it awkward and absurd. Nehru was not so blunt, but he had told Gandhi that he did not agree with *Hind Swaraj*. He had the advantage of working with Gandhi, so he had, over the years, adjusted to Gandhi's awkwardness. My generation had seen Nehru in the news clips they used to show before starting a movie. He looked tall and handsome, and pleasant like the background music of those black-and-white documentaries. In contrast, most children of my era knew Gandhi as a stiff stone statue standing in the public park with his stick. I was lucky to have spent my primary years at a Gandhian school, absorbing the warmth of a creative routine. That, however, did not help absorb the shock of *Hind Swaraj* when I read it years later.

---

* M.K. Gandhi's *An Autobiography* published by Penguin Books with Introduction and Notes by Tridip Suhrud, 2018, p. 591.

Its vision of India's future made little sense to me. I couldn't have laughed at it because it was Gandhi's. *Hind Swaraj* criticized everything that made life somewhat comfortable. It criticized trains and doctors, lawyers and parliamentary democracy. You can say it spares nothing. Its style and sweeping arguments were more than I could take despite my respect for Gandhi. *Hind Swaraj* was something one had to ignore. But now I enjoy its extremism, its radical critique of modern life. We have now seen it all—flyovers, SUVs, airport glitz and the glory of military might. We will soon have a bullet train; its silent shimmer will help us live under the debris of democracy.

Though the message of *Hind Swaraj* is harsh, its tone stays soft and slow throughout the long dialogue it presents between a reader and the editor of a newspaper. The conversational style is quite like Gandhi's letters and other writings—relaxed, patiently listening and arguing, with examples and metaphors from everyday life. References to the past are made to draw evidence. Despite this kind of reassuring movement, the text makes a peculiarly severe impact on us as readers. No logic that justifies common beliefs—about progress, democracy, government or anything else—appears to stand in the face of relentless, persuasive rejection. Apparently, *Hind Swaraj* hides its aggression and anger under a gentle veneer. It is one man's manifesto against a world constituted of violence and falsehood, for transforming it to save it. Its message is that India would have to set an example, but it can do so only after it transforms itself, by achieving true *swaraj* or a system that enables individuals to rule over themselves. The little book shines a magic mirror on its author. It shows that the man who shunned and abhorred violence and taught us to be tolerant was an impatient radical whose pleasant demeanour served as a means to draw people towards him and direct them away from worn-out ways. His real self was buried under layers of the image we thrust upon him.

Gandhi was halfway through his life when he wrote *Hind Swaraj*. The dismissive attitude, carefully camouflaged under a long quasi-dialogue, makes one wonder if Gandhi was a split personality: an apostle of non-violence in his public self, seething with all-encompassing anger in his deeper, personal self. His permanently upset inner self stayed with him to the end. He controlled it with the help of faith and by remaining committed to engaged communication with countless friends, strangers and rivals. In his famous and insightful obituary, Orwell said that Gandhi lacked humanism because he committed few sins and stayed saintly most of the time. It is a mixed verdict. Orwell must have felt uncomfortable with the lonely man who lived with all-round indignation over things the world had accepted as signs of progress—from the motorcar to the atomic bomb.

The regime Gandhi imposed on himself was woven around health. In *Hind Swaraj*, he ridiculed doctors, especially their fame as experts who protect others from illness. He was full of doubt about the efficacy of modern medicine and the science it was supposedly based on. One of his charges against doctors was that they profit from people's inability to overcome bad habits. His autobiography is replete with episodes that demonstrate how he hated and never failed to suspect the medicine prescribed by a doctor. Gandhi's suspicion foreshadows the nexus that is now so visible between doctors and the pharmaceutical industry. The numerous episodes of his refusal to take medicine can be read as instances of his obsession with nature's cure—both auto-healing and natural medicines. These episodes also provide testimony to his concept of health—as an aspect of faith in the spirit that keeps the body alive. The faith demands a sense of duty towards the body as God's gift, too precious to be outsourced to someone else's care. How can a doctor know my body better than me, Gandhi appears to ask. The confidence he showed while refusing to accept medical advice and while nursing someone sick could only have come from his religious faith. Call it idiotic or insane if you must. Towards the end of life, he wrote a small book on health. It explains the miracles one can achieve by looking after one's health and ailments, with self-awareness and confidence. These were, along with self-control, elements of Gandhi's pursuit of autonomy or freedom from dependence on a doctor for maintaining one's health. Doctor-assisted living is rejected as an intrusion into individual freedom and confidence. Seen this way, the critical remarks he makes on doctors in *Hind Swaraj* don't look as eccentric.

Hind Swaraj has a brief discussion of education. Although a separate chapter is devoted to it, the commentary does not go beyond a general critique of colonial education. There is not even a hint of the proposal Gandhi was to give twenty-seven years later for the Nai Talim. This startles me because handicrafts were the core of Nai Talim and Gandhi had already incorporated crafts into the routine of Tolstoy Farm in South Africa. I suppose my disappointment with the chapter on education in *Hind Swaraj* also had to do with my own primary schooling. The exciting school K. and I had attended as children were run along the lines Gandhi had proposed under Nai Talim. I wondered if he had simply forgotten his own experience of craft work at Tolstoy Farm while writing *Hind Swaraj*? Also missing from it is any direct reference to John Ruskin whose appreciation for manual crafts had impressed Gandhi. He had read Ruskin's *Unto This Last* when he was well-settled in his career in South Africa. Ruskin figures in the reading list given in *Hind Swaraj*, but his iconoclastic economics finds no mention. When I pondered on this absence, I recognized something wider: the absence of Gandhi's personal struggle and success in South Africa. *Hind Swaraj* makes no use of the lessons he had learnt—lessons that proved so fruitful for his campaigns in India. I realized that *Hind Swaraj* was a distraction, but a significant one.

A secret is buried underneath its skeletal text. Its message did not impress anyone, it seems, except the author himself. It must have given him the self-confidence he badly needed to jump into the sea of expectations awaiting him in his motherland. The story of its genesis is well known. The entire text was written by hand over a few days on a steamer. He had boarded it in London after a short visit there, heading for South Africa. His legal victories and public campaigns in that country had given him the identity of a fighter for justice. The role he foresaw playing in his homeland could hardly have been clear in his mind. In real-time, he was still five years away from leaving South Africa for good. He knew, however, that his fame as a fearless fighter had reached India. He was forty—a mature man, both excited and daunted by the impending future. He knew India as home, though not as the vast country he was about to lead. Aboard an ocean liner, he might have been looking for a message in the waves, on the horizon and in the sky. He needed sharp, urgent, somewhat loud answers to his questions. As a devout person who had achieved impossible victories against a hard adversary, he had his own reasons to believe that his wishes and vision would resonate with a higher entity.

Several biographers have noted that Gandhi wrote continuously for nine days. When his right hand got tired, he wrote with the left. He was writing in his mother tongue. The longhand draft in Gujarati covered some 267 pages—about thirty thousand words. Not much was altered or revised later. It looks as if he was gripped by the urge to write down all that had filtered into a shape in his mind. The venue and the process of writing leave no doubt that he felt driven. It would not be wrong to call it a poetic moment though the product was prose. The genre was that of a dialogue between two voices: one he called an editor's, the other that of a reader. For someone who spoke throughout his life of an inner voice guiding him, the two voices joining, in what became a lengthy tutorial, can only be described as benign instruments of self-excavation for seeking clarity. This could hardly be a considered choice of genre. It looks like a gift put into his hands in the middle of an ocean. His favourite book of dialogue, the Gita, was concerned with clarification, by divine power, enabling an afflicted, paralyzed warrior to overcome his doubts and get on with what he was supposed to do. *Hind Swaraj* is also preoccupied with clarifying doubts in a pedagogic mode of questions and answers. The one who asks persists with his arguments, and the one who responds is sure of convincing the other.

Hind Swaraj carries a list of books at the end. Each of the titles in this list had brought Gandhi closer to finding his own truth—his way of facing life and the world. Some of the books were about the difficulties that dependence on machines creates for ethical conduct; some others were about the human quest for the divine; the rest were about social and political responsibilities which the awakened citizen must accept. All these ideas had given Gandhi a psychological shelter. What he needed now was to make a fully worked-out statement of his own agenda. *Hind Swaraj* is the statement he makes to himself. He uses it to clear all his doubts—the ones he felt now and also the ones he anticipated. The text was to serve as a home where his inner being could live comfortably, surrounded by the currents of history that no one could stop. The arguments that the little book so densely records are like the short flights of a bird who lives on a ship. After each flight, it returns to the ship, its island home. Surdas, the blind fifteenth-century poet and among Gandhi's favourites, whose popular verses celebrate the beauty and generosity of Lord Krishna, had asked in a famous lyric: 'Where else should my mind find comfort? It's like the bird whose home is on a ship, so it returns to it again and again . . .'

Just as it served as an island where he had a permanent source of shelter, *Hind Swaraj* offers us a remote place to visit and marvel at its unbridled vehemence whenever we find the frantic movement of the established pattern of life unendurable. It offers an exotic kind of peace, with fury cloaked by unreasonable argument. The cerebral drama enacted in a tug-of-war format allows us to change places between the Reader who often argues the way we might, and the Editor who knows he will prevail because he keeps the overall frame of the conversation in his firm grip. The Editor cannot be questioned on fundamentals, so to say, simply because he has the longer vision that the Reader lacks. The distant disaster that is waiting to happen is all too close as far as the Editor is concerned. If indeed he represents Gandhi, we don't need to bow to him as a messiah. Rather, we enjoy his company during a holiday from the real world. The ship on which Gandhi wrote the book becomes our island too. It lets us criticize without the restraint that others—with whom we must live in a horrifying, worsening world—expect us to exercise. We are offered a brief sojourn in a new world. It encourages us to practice brazen contempt for reality and to liberate ourselves from the burden of history. No longer facing the need to make accommodations for a historical sense of reality, we feel light. We feel free of guilt too—the guilt of deliberately avoiding evil company, deliberately choosing to surround ourselves with goodness. The stronger of the two men who talk in the book seems to have his highest energy released by the location—a ship surrounded by oceanic waves.

II

Violence—any kind of violence—is an exercise of power. It inflicts suffering. I first saw that happen when our housemaid was thrashed. It was an early winter evening. I had been waiting for K. to bring the used tennis ball we used to bounce against the wall or just toss back and forth. For some reason he was late. The sun was about to set. There were no passers-by. Not far from where I was standing was a public staircase which connected the lower road to the one atop an old bridge. A wall stood on both sides of the staircase. Someone coming up remained invisible till the moment they reached the top. The wall ensured that the climber wouldn't notice anyone lurking at the top. That's where our maidservant's husband was hiding. He had a hockey stick with him. The moment his wife emerged from the staircase and put her foot on the upper road, the man struck her hard. I saw her fall to the ground, but he didn't stop. He hit her again and again. I used to see her almost every day. She used to come twice, to wash the dishes and do other chores. The heavy silver she wore on her feet and around her neck fascinated me. Sometimes she let me touch the two ornaments and trace the carving on them with my little fingers. When the hockey stick struck her for the first time, she screamed. Then she turned into a motionless heap after receiving several blows. A stream of blood trickled from her pulped, silent body.

Can I recall how I felt? Even in a film or on TV, a violent scene has a numbing effect. You forget about everything else and just stare as if all you have are eyes and they are too shocked to keep in touch with your mind, or perhaps the heart. This was my first encounter with brute force being showered on a human being—a woman I was fond of. The scene was etched on my memory, with the aftershocks that kept me awake all night long. An old man now, I still dread letting that scene haunt me. Forgetting it would be nice, but all you can do is push it back into the cupboard. There it stays, telling me something precious about violence: if you suffer it yourself, you just suffer, and cope—with help from an instant desire to avenge. Witnessing violence is quite different. It marks a breakdown of the belief one is born with that the world is an orderly, generally sensible place. Fear of what might happen—anything can—is part of learning about power—that only power can keep that fear down. The urge to seek power, to keep it ready in your closet, helps to live with fear. It can never be controlled fully; nor can you ever return to the state you were in before your eyes saw cruelty in action.

Unlike truth, non-violence has little threat value. An evil-minded person can suddenly get nervous if someone says to him, 'I know what you've been doing and I'm now going to reveal the truth.' Quite often such a threat slows down the villain. Prima facie, no real power resides in non-violence. In some famous episodes of his political career, Gandhi was able to use non-violence as a warning. It worked because his adversaries had had previous experience of his politics.

The English got used to Gandhi's approach to this matter. They realized that they couldn't sit back in the face of *satyagraha*. They were always prepared to use brute force. When you read history, it sounds unreal—that Gandhi's stature and strength grew incrementally with each episode of encounter with the State's violence. It sounds too good to be true. If brute power can be offset so nicely, who needs to raise armies? That might be a valid question, except that it is based on a rather shallow awareness of the past. There was nothing facile about the way Gandhi designed and implemented his plan of peaceful, passive resistance. Nor was there much hype. The key was defiance: declared defiance. How dare you do that, that is, say you'll break the law at such and such time and place, and then you go ahead. That's Gandhi's special screenplay.

By present day standards, Gandhi's discussion of violence in *Hind Swaraj* feels tepid. The chapter 'Brute Force' discusses why non-violent responses to wrong doings may be more effective than strategies involving violence. The style is leisurely, and the text is full of proverbs and allusions to common experience. The context is British power, but the treatment covers a wide range of examples of encounters with immoral behaviour, ranging from theft to life-threatening brutality. In the end, you feel a good case has been made for eschewing violence *as much as possible*, mainly because the gains made with the help of physical aggression do not last. Moral advocacy sustains this practical reason throughout the argument, but practical reasoning remains in the foreground.

It is only in the next chapter, 'Passive Resistance', that the moral superiority of non-violence, in addition to its strength, is fully asserted. This chapter is the heart of *Hind Swaraj*. It presents both the philosophy and its pithy defence. Gandhi preferred to call it satyagraha—literally, assertion of truth. For some reason, he felt its rendering in English as passive resistance was inaccurate. The opposite may be true because the English term conveys tenacity—of a deep-rooted vine or tree—that satyagraha doesn't. Be that as it may, the discussion does not reveal all that much concerning Gandhi's outright rejection of violence as a bad idea. Unless you are a devotee of Gandhi, you may not always feel sure that his rejection was always right. Also, these two chapters of *Hind Swaraj* and all the other bits and pieces scattered in Gandhi's voluminous texts, letters and speeches do not furnish a sufficient basis to convince us that human life and the world can do without violence.

As an idea, violence doesn't seem necessarily bad or odious. Its occasional necessity is universally acknowledged. If you are the one inflicting violence, you might feel justified. Teachers and parents who beat children often say it will serve a good purpose. I am sure my maid's husband would have defended his cruel action. People who beat their wives are quite loquacious with their justifications. British colonialists amply defended racist theories that called for the conquest and improvement of the vanquished. As for the conflict between nations, Gandhi did not mind participating in the war effort in different roles. Gandhi could not even avoid personal violence when he was young. In moments of anger, he hurt others intimately dependent on him. You can see these episodes as significant moments in his journey towards the realization that violence results from an uncontrollable impulse. His struggle to achieve total control of impulses belongs to a tradition of culture and ethics, but it does not necessarily make him an attractive figure.

Revenge against an individual who has wronged you is one thing; it is quite a different feeling when you feel that a whole community has trespassed on what you feel makes up the territory of rights belonging to your community. Then, a single person, even a boy or girl, becomes a representative, in your eyes, of the trespassers. Since your childhood, you have imbibed the correctness of social distance between castes, especially the upper ones and the lowest that are not even recognized as a part of the social order. The distance has enabled you to feel good and lucky about your status and disdain for the distant. When you find someone from the socially distant group within arm's reach one fine day, and moreover you know that he or she has made some mistake for which he deserves to be punished, you lose all self-control . . .

The salt satyagraha has become so symbolic, that it is seldom told as a real story. Nehru has given a glimpse of what it might have felt like. It was as though a spring had suddenly been released. Louis Fischer also captured the excitement, but the various narratives don't add up to what was a mini epic of passive resistance. One might ask: 'Was it passive?' Gandhi gave a special sense to this word. Hit me and my associates and feel damned for your sins, he appears to say. He had by this time acquired mastery over the politics of suffering. Its goal was to arouse guilt in the oppressor's heart. Let him exercise his legal right to act with aggression and violence; then alone he will recognize his fall. The way Gandhi organized the salt march reveals his management strategy. It lay in trust—of no one person over another. An Alexander would argue that for a sure victory, you need trusted lieutenants. In Gandhi's army, everybody was equally trustworthy, and this was no secret. Stunning success though it was, salt-making at the sea inaugurated a difficult decade for Gandhi.

* * *

A debate had started between K. and I when we were adolescents. It never ended. It was about effort—or rather, about when it is worth making an effort. How do you judge the worth of an effort *unless you make it first*, I used to argue. Life is too short

for that, K. would counter-argue. He never changed his mind
on this. He still doesn't think that a battle has its own moral
worth, so it shouldn't matter so much whether it is winnable.
He believes one must choose or be prepared to waste a lot of
energy and earn a lot of despair. In our teens we fought over
this, with our freshly acquired penchant for philosophy, me
taking the Gita line, K. a quasi-management view. Both of us
had seen a staged version of Lord Krishna's life, which included
his Gita discourse. We even knew the Sanskrit couplet where
Lord Krishna asks us to stop worrying about the results of our
action. K. didn't agree with it; I can't say that I understood it,
but *karma* as duty was my line in our debate. Wasteful effort is
a waste of time, he used to say. If you know that the problem is
chronic and complex, you should apply your mind and energies
to something more doable, K. argued. I can hear him say: 'Does
the Gita ask us to waste our energies? Does it ask us to compete
with God and fight every battle, like Don Quixote?'

Munna must be hallucinating, I thought as I
read this long para. This was not the only
part of the text where I had this suspicion,
but in this one he seemed to have gone a bit
too far, giving an impression of me that
I find uncomfortable. Who is not cynical
in adolescence? No doubt, Munna was more
idealistic, but his memory exaggerates my
position. He uses it to make Gandhi look
like Don Quixote and says so, and then
justifies it. Should I drop this bit, I
wondered. I felt painfully sorry that I
couldn't talk to him and straighten out
his memory of our youthful debate. Better
judgement prevailed when I argued with

myself that his affection for me let him
use me as a strong peg while engaging with
Gandhi with so much despair and anger to
fight within his own heart.

It doesn't feel right to say this, but nowadays I wonder if
Gandhi had a bit of Don Quixote in him. Gandhi's successes
in South Africa and during the initial years in India tempted
him to expand the list of his battles. He became a bit like Don
Quixote. The list expands further in the 1930s, with poverty
and the village economy on his mind. And a very sticky aspect
of culture, untouchability, too. How could he not see that
Ambedkar knew more about it because he had experienced it? I
also wonder why Gandhi took so long to get it—and still didn't
quite. His attention turned towards untouchability during the
years following the Poona Pact. He was an upper-caste Hindu
himself and knew that Hinduism had this problem, but its
scale and depth hit him only during his travels across long
distances in the countryside. It was as if he, now, for the first
time, saw the everyday hell of untouchables' lives. He must have
angered Ambedkar by inventing the term *harijan*, which means
'children of God', for them. Ambedkar must have thought
that if they *were* the children of God, it was surely a Hindu
God who forced them to live wretched lives. It was typical of
Gandhi to treat every problem as if it were within his reach.
The methods he chose to resolve untouchability were not new:
persuading and mobilizing—funds and workers—and putting
moral pressure on upper-caste society through fasting. The
last means would also be to expiate himself as an upper-caste
participant in untouchability.

Violence is ingrained in the caste system that forms the iron
framework of Hindu society. One assumes that Gandhi was
aware of this, but there is no guarantee. Upper-caste men of

his time saw varna as a cultural heritage. There was no M.N. Srinivas to explain how *jati* is the real structure and varna an idea. Gandhi seems to have held no particular grudge against either for a long time—right up to the mid-1930s. Ambedkar's firm stand forced Gandhi to perceive the moral outrage of untouchability that the varna classification and the caste system perpetuate. Like all educated Indians, Gandhi believed that the caste system would gradually become accommodating. He thought that caste relations would gradually improve through a two-layered approach: persuading the upper and awakening the lower castes. 'Persuading' and 'awakening' are key words of the Gandhi canon. He believed avoiding conflict was crucial if reforms in Hindu society initiated by men like him were to be sustained. An incident in Kavitha village in Ahmedabad tells us how Gandhi thought about social change. When the untouchables of this village sent their children to the local school, upper-caste Rajputs attacked them. Gandhi advised the untouchables to shift elsewhere. In an article in his magazine, he asked his reformer colleagues, to speed up their efforts to instil self-worth among Harijans. Prosecuting the upper castes was anathema for Gandhi. His doctrine of non-violence implied a change of heart for harmony in the community and avoidance of the State's coercive authority.

It's a pity that Gandhi's autobiography stopped around 1920 when he was just past fifty, for his next two decades were full of action and commotion, achievements and failures. Had he decided to add some details of his life or work from 1934, they would have given us a better idea of the turmoil that his intimate encounter with untouchability created in him. But there is a metaphorical window through which we can see how shocked he felt, despite the common knowledge he had possessed—like every Hindu—of the innate social distancing attitude built in the religion. His comment on the 1934 Bihar earthquake reveals the earthquake within him. When thousands die in an earthquake, one normally feels sympathy for the victims. It is human to bow to nature's fury in such a situation. Even if some call it an act of God, no one justifies it on God's behalf. That's what Gandhi did, calling the earthquake divine punishment for the practice of untouchability. How can you go so low, God might be saying to humanity, in this verdict. Now if God is omniscient or all-knowing, He must have been aware of the doctrine of caste and the practice of untouchability all along. How could it shock Him? Clearly, it was Gandhi who had suffered a shock—by noticing the scale of untouchability and its meaning in the lives of its victims. The shock was so great that he found in the earthquake, and its terrifying effects, evidence of God's anger.

Let us go a step further. Was the shock so great that it made Gandhi wonder about his pronouncement of Indian civilization's moral superiority over all others? His *lex divina* view of the earthquake—as God's justice—was no emotional sigh of a believer saying, 'This is God's leela, what can one say about such things.' Rather, it is a devotee's endorsement of divine retribution for deeply disappointing human behaviour. We can only imagine the implications of Gandhi's disappointment. The young writer of *Hind Swaraj* had taken the view that Hinduism was originally free of social evils: but they had crept into it later. They could all be dealt with once India got rid of the crippling colonial rule and its civilizational assault.

Gandhi always viewed politics as a part of the broader work of social repair. Two slashes in the social fabric bothered him more than other numerous repair sites: Hindu–Muslim rancour and the practice of untouchability. Both have been discussed in *Hind Swaraj*, but something had changed within him since he composed that manifesto. He now had a better idea of the jagged edges of the torn tears. Untouchability had revealed its muddy depth, and the Hindu–Muslim divide—and the animosity sustaining it—was getting worse. He was still the undisputed leader of India's millions, but his grip on the direction of politics and the vast army of his followers was no longer convincing. His closest companions and well-wishers had died one by one: Mahadev Desai and Tagore in 1941, and Kasturba in 1944. Unabated Hindu–Muslim riots and the spectre of Partition were becoming fiercely real. Above all, he faced the aching discomforts of an ageing father figure no longer heeded in the family. He dared to walk alone, and had the tough resolve to cope with whatever came next, but coping has its limits. He gave up his wish to live long. The vale of tears drowning him pressed the apostle of patience to seek instant discharge from duty. And he got it.

Today, going through the second round of Hindu nationalist rule, we too are coping with deep disappointment. We had imagined that the essential character of our nation was settled. It had been articulated in the Constitution and we had believed that it was a matter of time for the spirit of this document to, with anticipated struggles over several issues, become reality—that of a secular, progressive republic. Its greatest attainment, in our eyes, was how different it was from its neighbour, Pakistan. Over time, we would impress Pakistan to emulate us. Then its hostility would simmer down, especially over Kashmir.

It feels like a bruised, broken dream. We are becoming more and more like Pakistan. An incredible idea until now. We can't miss the details that testify to the truth of this bizarre thought. Our dilemma is awful—how to admit the truth even as it strides towards becoming reality. It is early in the twenty-first century still and a growing mass has gathered around a late-nineteenth-century notion of India. What we had assumed to be fringe, arrogantly sits centre-stage. We first believed people would reject it; when it started gaining popular support, we said people were being manipulated; we now feel people have disappointed us, that they would have to be reawakened. We see nothing wrong in ourselves—we, the thoughtful, who were pushing India forward, keeping in mind its image fashioned during the freedom struggle. Those who did not struggle against colonial rule are now in office, managing the State that we had run for so long that we got accustomed to steering it and to believing that we alone could manage it properly.

Nothing inspires us now. Our fighting spirit has run dry; our nationalism looks woolly, sitting beside what is on display—in war museums, tourist centres, with towering statues and poles on top of which the tricolour flies in universities and marketplaces. We are stunned by the audacity of the new ruling culture—its crassness, its stuffy preachiness, its fakery. We are smitten by our defeat, struck by our irrelevance.

The creators of Pakistan have been proved right. Warmongering is now a permanent routine. Advocacy of peace is seen as a sign of weakness. The atmosphere is reminiscent of post-Partition days when suspicion and fear between Hindus and Muslims ran deep. His prayer meetings at Birla House had started in the April of 1947, and he continued till the last day of his life—he was assassinated before he could speak. At these meetings, Gandhi responded to the news coming from different cities and regions. He conveyed his counsel and message with the patience he had practised throughout his adult life. The speeches he delivered evening after evening comprise a voluminous document, celebrated and precious because it contains his last public addresses. They are special because they carry the evidence of his awareness that his listeners were unhappy, and at times angry and hostile. He could hardly expect to satisfy them with his repetitious advice for maintaining peace and good sense. The published texts of these speeches are not resplendent with inventive similes and metaphors drawn from everyday life, applied to draw the listeners' attention to a focal point. These familiar features of his style are rare in these evening speeches. The sentences are lucid, at times prolix and laden with an unspoken commitment to a responsibility that had become one-sided, conveying his awareness that the audience—the people he had always turned to for seeking inspiration and ideas—could no longer play this role. They were at the venue to hear him say something, nothing more.

The doctor had run out of remedies to prescribe. The ones he had prescribed in the past were no longer efficacious, and he had no new ones to offer. He wanted to heal, making each passing moment a test of his ability to endure failure, without loss of faith. His inner self wherein lived the voice he had often mentioned as guiding him was in pain, exuding relentless bewilderment. His dialogue with God isn't hard to put into words:

'Where did I go wrong, Lord?'

'Why do you feel so sure that you went wrong?'

'Why else do I suffer?'

'So, you're looking for a cause of your suffering?'

'Yes.'

'I can see you're suffering, but I don't know the reason.'

'I thought you know everything . . . nothing is hidden from you.'

'Except what is hidden in the human mind.'

A startled, somewhat confused Gandhi pauses. After a few seconds, he starts again.

'In that case, let me tell you that I suffer because I have failed.'

'But you always knew that success and failure are not in your hands—you've read the Gita: "You can only try . . ." And that you did.'

'In all sincerity, Lord.'

Gandhi's voice became feeble as he said, after a pause,

'People believed in me, in my sincerity . . . they were sure of my success.'

'Aren't they pleased that you got them freedom?'

'But I wanted freedom with unity.'

God appeared to smile before saying, 'You believe you can control everything.'

It was not a question, but it stopped Gandhi for several breaths. Then he said,

'I was wrong to think like that. I know you control everything. Why did you let it happen?'

'So, you wanted me to control everything and leave no room for people to learn from their doings?'

Gandhi stopped again. He thought he should try again after a few days, but he knew from experience that dialogue with God couldn't be planned in advance. He had heard God's voice several times earlier, calling it his inner voice. Each time, he heard it at an unanticipated moment, setting him on a course of action, like the Salt March. But this moment was different. He was facing an inner crisis, a sense of despair, a loss of hope—something he had no experience of. Even in the darkest patches of his long career, he hadn't let hope slip away.

Like him, we are coping these days with a failed dream. In the first two decades of his struggle for India's freedom, the Partition was not even a passing thought. When it happened, it broke his heart, but his spirit was still alive. He wanted to walk to Pakistan. What difference that would have made one can't say. Counterfactuals don't always help. Had Rajiv Gandhi not opposed the Shah Bano verdict, had he not ordered the unlocking of the old temple at Ayodhya, would that have averted India's sharp political turn to the right? Such tempting thoughts always conceal a hundred facts and make history look simpler.

* * *

Fighting untouchability was just one of the many episodes of his life where Gandhi appears to have competed with God—though impelled by God himself, he would have said in his defence. There is another way to sort this out. Gandhi had come face to face with evil several times, but he was also unacquainted with its myriad other forms and shapes. His advice to the citizens of Hiroshima was vacuous. They should have prayed for the pilot who dropped the bomb. Like millions, then and now, Gandhi thought of the nuclear bomb as an explosive, somewhat stronger than others. He didn't know that the thousands who were fatally charred within seconds had no time to sense their death, let alone to pray. Nor did those who ran amok while their bodies burnt, like the shadowy figures in Dante's *Inferno*.

The urge to injure or kill is innate to the human heart; the mind can't always control it. The form this urge takes in a war is rather different, and it also depends on the war itself, that is, who is fighting whom. We assume that Gandhi was against all wars because they were violent. That was perhaps not true. In fact, he was not averse to fulfilling war-time duties of various kinds, including nursing. His doctrine of non-violence offers ways to avoid, or at least put off violence, but does not cover war as such, although his style of politics does indicate how we can bypass, or at least postpone, a war. He was in his seventies when the Second World War and Hiroshima atomic bombing took place. His response to the two doesn't impress.

Dachau and Hiroshima mark two faces of the same war, but they are starkly different. The suffering inflicted on Hiroshima was instant and intense, but most probably it didn't originate from chronic hatred. Dachau and other German 'concentration camp' sites present a contrast to Hiroshima and Nagasaki, in more than one way. Hitler's killing industry was fuelled by the politics of hate that had a much longer history than the war itself. The cruelty and suffering that the concentration camp sites like

Dachau commemorate went on and on—for nine long years, to be precise. One can safely surmise that Gandhi had no real idea of what actually happened at Hiroshima or in the German death camps. Of course, he knew that Hitler was a dictator and said so, but then, what went on in the concentration camps was not a mere dictator's act. The fact that Gandhi wrote him a letter—the British censored it—tells us how ignorant he was, and how innocent too. This he would have acknowledged had he lived long enough to visit Dachau or Auschwitz as a tourist. The silence pervading the barracks, the crematoria and the medical experimentation rooms would have stunned him out of his assumption that Hitler could have reformed himself and attained redemption.

About the atomic assault on Japan too, he thought in terms that people who have not visited Hiroshima continue to think to this day. These are terms derived from other kinds of bombings. Gandhi's statement that the citizens of Hiroshima could have prayed for the bomber pilot before they perished conveys his inability to grasp Hiroshima. It was a reasonable limitation. The world has moved on. Education and media have ensured that Hiroshima will not be grasped well enough to fuel anxiety over nuclear bombs and energy. John Berger quipped that the world needs to forget Hiroshima 'so that more nuclear bombs can be made'.

A museum was built on the site where the bomb fell in Hiroshima. The entrance gallery had panoramic pictures depicting the immediate hell that erupted. One showed three children whose hair was aflame and whose eyes carried a message: 'Don't try to understand what happened to us here.' As you walked on, you saw several more frozen images of excruciating suffering. These pictures have now been removed. Within seconds, the American bomber had flown away to safer skies. His escape manoeuvre must have been part of his training to accomplish this first-ever act of inflicting a holocaust on common people. Those pictures have been removed forever. American tourists didn't appreciate them, the chief curator of the Hiroshima Museum told me.

Sincere servants of the State would do anything to comply with orders. Their sense of duty overrides their conscience. Thomas Merton's comment on the German concentration camps startles us because we want to believe that the officers deployed there were evil-minded. Not at all, says Merton, they were routine observers of assigned duties. Aren't we all in our work lives? As a civil servant of the highest cadre, I can't quarrel with Merton's conclusion. The Emergency that Indira Gandhi had imposed in 1975 amply proved this. In the German case, the officers had contempt for the victims too. Call it hatred in the deep freezer of culture and history. Any competent populist leader can raise the freezer's temperature to allow congealed emotions to flow and spill warm blood.

* * *

It was summer. I was home for a long holiday. K. and I spent all day—except the late afternoons—together. Long before the sun got hot, we went on our bicycles to Kundeshwar. I rode my shining new Atlas cycle; K. was on his old Hind with a rattling chain cover. At Kundeshwar, we swam in the river we had known so well from our primary school days. In May, the riverbed was mostly dry, but the mossy spillway gave it some depth. There was hardly anyone else at that hour. Sitting at the river's edge, swimming, drying ourselves—we talked non-stop. There was so much in our separate lives to talk about. I didn't know how bad and heartless some of K.'s teachers were; he had no idea of the tight regime I had to follow in Scindia's hostel, how dull the food was, and what it meant to be homesick now and then.

Junior Division NCC drill took K. away to school every afternoon. NCC had become compulsory in government schools and colleges after the Chinese invasion of 1962. While K. stamped out his left-right-left, I spent the long sweaty afternoons sunk in an old cane sofa, browsing through abridged versions of Scott and Dickens—illustrated hardbacks that my father had read in his teens. I sat on the street-side veranda; it was somewhat airy and allowed you to peep through a lattice wall and see who was walking by.

One day I spotted K.'s mother and shouted 'Aunty!' She stopped as I stepped out. Being a principal, she had no holidays. We walked to her door and went in. She sat me down and gave me the nice stuffed paratha that she had made for K. Just before the exams, my history teacher had covered the chapter on the Independence and Partition. He had mentioned the names of cities where Hindu–Muslim riots had occurred. The name Lahore rang a bell. Aunty had told me once how beautiful it was, with a river and a fort and a canal flowing through a long luxurious park. This picture didn't gel with riots, so I asked, 'Aunty, were you in Lahore during the Partition?'

It was merely one of my dozen-a-day questions, but it took Aunty by surprise. For a few moments, she stared at me. She was tired. Her affection for me and the heat and the silence in the room did something to her. I can still see her round face and greying hair, khadi sari with a blue border, as she sat rigid, looking at me, talking. Memories poured out, her voice changed, her eyes looking past me towards the wall, the window, nowhere. She told me how K.'s father escaped death, twice, attempting to get back to Mian Mir, the part of Lahore where his law office was, hoping to retrieve his books and other documents. He was forced to turn back halfway; flames all around and people running, falling; his turning around meant more scenes like that, and by this point, Aunty was close to sobbing. She paused, made me promise not to say a word of what I had heard to K., ever. Then she talked a little more, about how she had crossed the border and spent a fortnight in a camp, not knowing if her husband had survived. Before she stopped, she said K. knew nothing of all this—and he should never learn anything.

That was my first lesson of the Partition. A second, much longer lesson came when my history teacher at St. Stephen's drew its historical contours and recommended several sources and a novel, *Train to Pakistan*. A lot of books have been written over the decades about the Partition and what its victims went through. You often come across the word 'holocaust' in the descriptions of Partition. It is so misleading. People killed and injured other people; in contrast, the German holocaust was a State-ordered killing. How can the two be compared? Marching men and women into gas chambers bears no resemblance to the one-at-a-time stabbing and raping of thousands. History flattened to numbers alone loses all traces of meaning. Statistics, narratives, even photographs mean little if inheritors of a violent past are educated to see it as a mass frenzy. Of course, the Partition's violence was that, but it was more than that as well—an expression of one last wish before those you want to leave their homes. Their fate was already sealed, yet so many of them had to be killed as well and their women folk raped before they were captured or killed or all of the above.

We are stuck in the Partition. We relieve ourselves by thinking—as Gandhi, his associates, his adversaries did—that the division was illegitimate, morally wrong, an administrative mistake, most probably a conspiracy. It gives us reason to continue in our neighbourly hatred, while the neighbour continues to give us plentiful reasons to sustain our distrust and loathing. They are necessary spices to make patriotism tasty in the age of consumerism. The political purposes of

Partition's memory are best served by memorializing it as an act of betrayal, by the outgoing British in collusion with Muslim leaders. But the Partition's politics go back further. Mumtaz Shah Nawaz traces its blossoming in the late 1930s, in the title of her autobiographical novel, *The Heart Divided*. Her book amplifies the known historical facts of the period by tracing the small details of everyday life in the north with the patience of a diarist. As the story develops, we get deeper glimpses into the lives of three young Muslim women, noticing the changes in life around them. Seen through their eyes, the last ten years of India's freedom movement present a struggle between two nationalisms. History since Partition has proved the veracity of this perception. Neither of the two nationalisms has managed to adjust to the other. Dreams of decisive violence persistently appear in both, making Gandhi's officially recognized martyrdom for the cause of peaceful co-existence a distant occurrence.

Between the two national projects sits the festering body of Kashmir. Talking about it is full of risk now, like everything else. Retired officers who devoted their careers to Jammu and Kashmir shift to whispering when the subject arises. Injuring hundreds of young people in the eye with pellet guns goes without comment. Who can afford to say a word? Pursed lips mark the new style of governance. Kashmir has bled for a long, long time, and it now attracts nobody's attention. Violence, its threat and its utility as the only means to ensure peace is the authorized truth.

Basharat Peer narrates story after story of brute force used on Kashmiri people. He calls his childhood a *Curfewed Night*. It reminds us of Gandhi's theory of violence—that it can only be understood and dealt with at the level of the individual human being. The term 'mass' leader is rightly used to describe his political personality, but it does little justice to Gandhi, the teacher. His pedagogy treated each person as being different and as important as anyone else. Gandhi was surely aware of the hysteria that can turn a crowd into a violent machine. In fact, he did create hysteria in his audience on many occasions, except that it was a positive hysteria if such a term can be allowed. People felt stirred by his words and manner of speaking; they felt compelled to do something that might serve his cause or make him happy. When millions are involved, there must be a great diversity of impulses. Despite Gandhi's advocacy, non-violence didn't become a reliable, popular impulse. Its adversary was always lurking around. Gandhi just didn't stop condemning violence, and when savagery broke out unstoppably, he sacrificed himself. It consoles us that someone cared that much—for us, our sanity.

We challenged him then, and we do so now, more vigorously. We had learned something, but we let it go. Nasty, cheap-talking leadership eroded our soul. It is not a usual time in history when rulers take to spreading hate. You need tens of thousands of hate mongers, mind numbers and determined distracters to finish off Gandhi's relics lodged in India's soul. To manage yelling armies, you need wicked commanders. Astonishingly, they have managed it all. That's why one says that India has changed.

Gandhi has been untraceably left behind, lost in the dust of a long battle. His key ideals—truth, non-violence—have been replaced by new conduct brands: fabrication and incitement. File fake cases, catch a few, bend the media—thereby, you finish off India's limited civil-intellectual stamina. Fear isn't difficult to inject in fifty-year-olds running households. Younger ones are easier to manage with unemployment and hope. This model of governance works miracles as it doesn't disturb democracy. Even bulldozers don't disturb. Crushing of contrary thoughts takes little force in the digital age. All its instruments are light and precise, and their delivery is foolproof.

Munna died a few months before the farmers' protest started. Had he lived to see its sustained momentum—to the day of success when the three new laws that the farmers opposed were withdrawn—he might not have felt that Gandhi has been left 'untraceably behind'. The farmers' protest had all the characteristics of satyagraha. Their leaders—localized and disparate though they were—stuck to their argument that the new laws would give big corporate players a strong foothold in agriculture. The government tried to stop them from reaching Delhi, used several threats to provoke them, but the farmers stayed peaceful. In their thousands they sat at the borders of Delhi, braving the bitter cold weather and rain for months. Some seven hundred died on the road. Nothing seemed to work to melt the stony heart of the government, but the farmers and their leaders didn't lose patience. Had Munna witnessed the movement, he would have seen an unmistakable stamp of Gandhi on it. Apart from demonstrating the true spirit of satyagraha, it also proved that the soul of India still lives on in its villages.

No one nowadays minds violence when the State opts for it. Western nations taught us to equip the State with weapons, and with laws that protect State functionaries when they resort to violence. Gandhi's critique of violence was a part of his critique of the State. Even with his colleagues, he got nowhere with his views on statecraft. That part of *Hind Swaraj* was treated as a joke: one more facet of a respectable, awkward man. When he was killed, the cremation rituals reflected no concern for his assiduously maintained distance from the State. He had held no office, had accepted no patronage from the State, colonial or Indian, but still, he received a State funeral. Aldous Huxley was troubled by the news of Gandhi's funeral—with full military honours, including cannons and warplanes. How could India be imagined as a nation without arming the State, the early nation-builders must have wondered. If there was some confusion, it was dispelled by the 1962 Chinese invasion. Then onwards, there was no looking back at the idea of swaraj. Gandhi's dream, that India would present a unique model of self-governing village communities, no longer made sense. It became a chant for bi-annual worship, scheduled on the days he was born and murdered.

Not just against external threats, the State had to be weaponized for contingencies against the masses as well. Colonialism was dead; long live the law-and-order State the English had assembled. Neither the Congress nor its adversaries thought much about this. Irrespective of their caste or class background, provincial chief ministers were held up as models when they improved law and order. No other priority mattered. No ministry mattered like home. When older offices showed signs of fatigue, new parts were added to the machine, for vigilance and enforcement. No one thought the augmented State would one day begin to bite Gandhi's party and democracy itself. With its symbols stolen and co-opted, the party is now trying to dye its jaded secularism in soft saffron shades. Under new, unhesitating hands, the State has shifted to better ways of aggressing—a tax raid here, a data demand there, for usable self-details. Who needs deep breathing, immunity from fear? We're all in it together. The poor are not, but they can be managed by digital transfers.

A State's efforts to maintain peace can never mitigate violence. The administration academy doesn't teach you that when you join civil service, you learn it quickly, nevertheless. With its monopoly over laws and the instruments of violence, the State can control any situation. In fact, it excels in creating situations where it can demonstrate its blunt powers to control. As people become more prone to State control, their capacity to live peacefully declines.

It's just like the old days. In a colony, people are seen as troublemakers. Someone must protect them from themselves. As officers, it's our job to choreograph public gatherings organized by political parties. Civil servants and the police force work together to manage the crowds mobilized by parties. Indian-style democracy would collapse without the district-level bureaucracy's participation in political theatre. But how can it collapse if it never stood on its own feet, Gandhi might have asked me, noticing my thoughts. Democracy's drama has depended on the State machinery's violent strength, he would have written in a revised edition of *Hind Swaraj*. And political parties have repeatedly manipulated the people in collaboration with the administration. I feel like asking: 'But, aren't you a little bit pleased that India has a functioning democracy?'

'After reading me all these months, do you still need to ask me? How can I be pleased with this democracy? Lakhs are without work, and when they gather to try their luck in recruitment *melas*, the police beat them with lathis.'

'That happens when they become unruly.'

'So, you admit that our youth are incapable of following rules although they have attended schools and colleges?'

'The problem is they all hanker after government jobs. That's why there are such unmanageable crowds.'

'You've been a civil servant, with privileges and security, so you know well why our young people aspire for government jobs . . . No private job can bring that kind of security. You can't blame them.'

I thought he might slip away any moment and I would lose the opportunity to ask a question buried in my heart for a long time. So, I diverted the delusion and said:

'Please don't go away . . . I want to know something. People turn violent ever so often these days. What is wrong with State violence if it quells such eruptions?'

Gandhi appeared to be startled as if to say how a retired officer could pretend that he didn't know the answer I had sought. He smiled. I heard him heave a long sigh.

'State violence is a sign . . . It shows the State's view that people don't know how to live their collective lives. It is the same old story. The British thought they were here to civilize the Indians. Now the Indian State thinks it's all right to use its might to force the people to be civil. It assumes they have no moral instincts left. Acting with such assumptions, the State can only deplete their moral resources further. You must have seen evidence of this depletion with your own eyes.'

'Yes, I think so, but please go on, sir,' I begged him.

'If a woman is being harassed and a passerby intervenes, the aggressors thrash him first. No wonder people don't intervene nowadays. A mob can lynch a man and passersby won't look in that direction. By the time the police arrive, he is dead.'

'But the courts do seek a report . . .' I heard myself say, in a voice close to choking.

'The story of courts is worse. They are unable to stop anything. They can't even stop hate speech. They hesitate to tell the police that its narrative is frivolous. Thousands are rotting in jails because judges can't expose the police. They realize that the police must enjoy impunity if law and order is to be maintained. The State's capacity for violence has terrorized truth to flee the nation.'

Gandhi's voice faltered, then disappeared, like a bad mobile connection. I felt lost and dismal, a dead tiger's eye watching me from the wall. It was a boyhood memory. Hunting was popular among the royals; a pill recommended for occasional use to alleviate boredom. Jungles were all around, with deer and their high-status predators, jackals and foxes, wild boars and bison. Every few weeks, my father and uncle, the King, got ready to spend two or three nights on a *machaan*. A dedicated team of drummers would accompany them when the target was a panther or a tiger. After unsuccessful expeditions, my father returned with a deer or two strapped to the roof of our Dodge. Twice during my primary school years, he returned with more substantial booty. The first time, it was a leopard and the second time a tiger. The open trunk is what I remember, with servants and neighbourhood urchins peering into it. Inside the trunk lay the cold striped body of a tiger on his side, with his eyes shut and his whiskers sprouting from his bony cheeks. I was a bit disappointed that I could not see his eyes. Within a few weeks, our drawing room had the stuffed head of the tiger mounted on a wooden plaque staring with glass eyes across the room at the head of a stag similarly mounted on the opposite wall, spreading sharp antlers and with large limpid glass eyes. The centre table stood, as usual, on a shiny deerskin spread across the middle of a Persian rug.

My father used to say that a tiger's eyes shine like light from a great distance in the dark jungle and that when you see those glowing eyes, you must not allow fear to grip you because that's the moment to get a firm grip on your gun and shoot. Listening to dad talk like this made me feel proud of him. My mind now feels crowded. I know my father was a good man, but was he brave? Questions like that assail me and I feel sick all over again. So, was the person who shot at a bare-chested old man walking with assistance brave? Some people think so. He had warned us, and for a while, we did listen to him.

Violence against girls and women continues unabated even as many demonstrate greater stamina for resistance. Revengeful attitudes towards young women who speak up or resist have emerged. To an extent, this is a consequence of education. An educated young woman must fight several simultaneous battles alone, like Abhimanyu, in the Mahabharata, who was surrounded by his enemies arrayed in strategic formation. This young hero of the Mahabharata knew how to negotiate this formation, but he had no help. Girls fighting for life and dignity feature in the news daily, but no episode can compare with the one in which a paramedical student in Delhi fought with her assailants inside a bus. One of them inserted in her body a steel rod with pointed teeth. In an older episode, a woman had faced—how else should one recall and describe?—a policeman walking along a crowd in a small town in western Uttar Pradesh. They couldn't charge him adequately; now, despite better-honed laws, girls must fear an encounter with brute force—anywhere, anytime. To saffron eyes, it's all due to evil Western influence.

The State protects—from discrimination and atrocities—the millions categorized as Scheduled Castes and Scheduled Tribes. Ambedkar knew that the special status endowed upon the untouchables in the Constitution would not suffice. His disagreement with Gandhi on the caste system was sharp. History has judged the matter in his favour. Had Gandhi lived for a few more years after independence as Ambedkar did, the two men might have come closer in their view of caste prejudice. Together they might have evolved a better strategy to counter it. My fascination for counterfactuals tires me at times. I know that prejudice is something far more stubborn than Gandhi might ever admit. In her *Mill on the Floss*, the Victorian novelist George Eliot explains that 'prejudices come as natural food of tendencies which can get no sustenance out of that complex, fragmentary, doubt-provoking knowledge which we call truth.' Gandhi would probably reject this view of truth.

Gandhi's advice to the lower castes of Kavitha village shows how mistaken he was—both in his understanding of caste violence and potential remedies for it. That was 1935. In the final phase of his life, Ambedkar felt uncertain about the efficacy of State protection of the untouchables. He eventually embraced the Buddha's vaster vision. His uncompromising style has sustained hope among India's Scheduled Castes, but their vulnerability has not diminished with time, nor has the upper-caste mind improved—in awareness or the sensibility required to shed stereotypes and prejudice. News of atrocities inflicted on Dalits, especially girls and women, comes in daily. The happy middle-class reader couldn't care less. Some Dalits now are visible members of the middle class. They perhaps feel a silent rage within. I have known many in offices who knew how to maintain psychic distance between their settled lives and the ones across the watershed. Individuation of justice has helped democracy survive, by leaving the caste system alone to maintain culture and its religious content.

The story of people we call 'tribal' is a bit different. Don't we all, including the proud middle class, deserve that label? Despite their modernity, nations also behave like tribes, ready to pick up their bows and arrows the moment they sense intrusion. In fact, most communities recognized as Scheduled Tribes are more civilized than most nations, including our own. I too held the usual stereotypes before my posting in a tribal district of eastern Madhya Pradesh. I was a greenhorn, with authority to do things, or so I thought. My agenda was the State's agenda—development at all costs. One day, an elderly Baiga couple visited me. They had learned that I had the power to stop things. Their village was barely thirty kilometres from the district headquarters, so I decided to accompany them and see for myself what they were talking about—they had complained of our forest officials and guards harassing them for collecting herbs in a reserved forest. It was a predominantly Gond village with a few Baiga families. The beautifully painted houses charmed me; so did the clean lanes. It was a contrast to the lanes of the district headquarters.

Gandhi found in tribal communities a model of village republics—self-governing, self-sufficient. It was a humble, respectful view of the tribal people. The shooting of Bastar's tribal king Praveer Chandra Bhanjdev marked the end of that respect. It was 1966, the peak of summer. Bhanjdev's fort was surrounded by armed police. The tribal soldiers carried bows and arrows. They had no chance to defend their Maharaja, a champion of tribal rights. He was fighting an already-lost battle. During my induction years in administration, his legend was often recounted and his death was remembered as an embarrassment for the government. But that mood passed into history despite officers like B.D. Sharma battling the system internally, demanding humane treatment and justice for the Scheduled Tribes. The hope of justice was receding as the wheels of development were gearing up for a faster, reckless drive. No one could stop or slow them down. Verrier Elwin, who guided Nehru's benign hopes and policies had died in the early spring of 1964. Nehru died that summer.

Adivasi is a better term to describe the tribes. It means the first or original inhabitants. That's why the saffron types don't like that term and prefer *vanvasi* or forest dwellers instead. Their reasoning is not hard to guess. What will happen to the

Aryans on whose indigenous status stands the edifice of saffron struggle against secular historians? For India to become fully Hindu, the tribes need to be proselytized into Hindu ways, deities and rituals. This missionary work is a massive saffron enterprise in different tribal belts, but especially in the North-east. There they resent the spread of Christianity, but in their overall perspective, they worry less about the exploitation of tribal communities than about their isolation from the so-called mainstream. Chhattisgarh offers the best example of consensus—between saffron and non-saffron rulers. Both groups supported the incredible policy of raising a tribal militia to fight the Maoists. Known as Salwa Judum, its mobilization intensified bloodshed. The State's goal across the central tribal belt has been clear—to vacate tribal occupation so the minerals beneath and the forests above the earth's surface can be smoothly exploited. There is strong corporate pressure as well. Unhesitating violence in tribal areas is a sordid chapter of post-Gandhi India. It takes many different forms; at times, using welfare as cover. Tribal girls are to be used for the trial of a commercial vaccine for cervical cancer, with the concerned bureaucrats acting as proxy parents, giving consent. An easy-to-translate, two-line poem by Jacinta Keriketta says it all: 'They are waiting for us to get civilized/ we are waiting for them to get human.' It is a pointless plea, to a system of in-built violence.

Gandhi had foreseen the crisis India's cultural strengths would face in its mutation into an industrialized quasi-Western country. Evicting the tribal people from their homelands was inescapable for this mutation. Civil servants of my generation—and several more—were taught to view post-eviction planning as the panacea for misery. Nowadays, eviction is an end by itself; the State sees little use for planning in any detail. Transformation is all it wants and in the shortest possible time. According to current liberal orthodoxy, once people are evicted, they would appreciate the benefits of life in shantytowns. They would soon learn to appreciate the new visionaries. Their children would study a new history in digital books. One great reformer of tribal communities says he will turn them into income taxpayers in one generation. The other visionaries expect them to embrace Hinduism. The battle for the soul of tribal belts is on.

I heard that a young Bengali was in town where I was posted as a collector in my early days. I called him for tea. 'I'm a Naxalite' he told me without hesitation. In those early days of the ideology, Naxalism was in fashion among highbrow Bengali young men. They flaunted it in prestigious colleges as a marker of social commitment. I said to my visitor, 'I'm glad you're here . . . See me whenever you need something.' He seemed surprised by my offer and laughed. We talked about the 'tribal problem' and Verrier Elwin's love for Madhya Pradesh. He told me how much he had enjoyed Elwin's study of the Baiga people. I was curious to know what he was doing in the district. He instantly turned vague. 'I can appreciate why you don't want to share your plans with a bureaucrat,' I reassured him, but he didn't feel at ease. Something had suddenly altered. Decades have passed and the world has changed, but I haven't figured out what altered this young visitor's mood and trust in me that afternoon. My best guess is that he felt I was mocking his 'plans' for the tribal people. He didn't like it. Young men of that time nursed big dreams for India's transformation through its original, uncontaminated inhabitants.

Then there is the ultimate case—of Muslims. I call it ultimate because no group has a comparable lack of hope. Muslims know what people like me don't want to accept. They knew India was changing; now they believe India has changed forever. Tell a Muslim that India will eventually recover; he will stare at you. My senior friend, Dr Malik, says: 'We've seen them all', meaning all parties. He knows the Pakistan project has also failed, so there's no point criticizing India. He takes a deep breath when I start a conversation. The corrupt, the frivolous, the social climbers, among the Muslims are happy. The Hindu Rashtra idea poses no threat to them. They are entrepreneurs, so they don't care. They'll survive a pogrom anywhere. Their business stays afloat, no matter what happens. Great guys of the kind the new India needs.

For others, the present is a hell that can only get worse. They were suspect, but they can now be openly despised. The government is determined to erase every trace of India's Muslim past, all Allahabads are in the waiting line for renaming. Things unknown are happening. Hate them, boycott their shops, demolish their houses—all this and more can be given out as an appeal. The term Islamophobia is often used to invoke a global context for what is happening in India. The global scenario has doubtless contributed to religious polarization in India, but the story of Indian Muslims and what they face today has a specificity of its own. Gandhi is described in school textbooks—still used in many states—as a martyr for the cause of Hindu–Muslim unity. Martyrdom suggests that he lost the battle he had chosen to fight. The fact that an inspired Hindu killed Gandhi clarifies that his espousal of the Muslim cause unsettled a darkened streak in India's ideological spectrum. That streak has now attained political and cultural power. We, the unhappy, must shed our tendency to show surprise over the ascent of disrespect for Islam. It was never a short story; the local lost-wax method of metal casting has acquired a toughening global mix. Islamophobia is both accurate and a misnomer. People are afraid of Muslims, and the fear enables them to enjoy guilt-free hatred. It's a nice fit.

Imagine a man looking for a room in a guesthouse. His wife in a black burka is with him. Only her eyes are visible, framed by a narrow strip. The receptionist must quickly decide whether to give a room to this Muslim couple. In those few moments, he must survey the triangle of business, safety and fairness. The receptionist is around forty—old enough to be familiar with global history and India's, during the past few decades. Above all else, he knows terrorism well. It is laminated on Islam. When secular truth-techies like me meet someone like this receptionist, we try scratching away the laminated surface of his limited outlook by pointing out that there are many non-Muslim terror outfits in the world. We get nowhere. Self-distancing is the first reflex that the sight of a Muslim arouses in an ordinary Hindu's mind these days. A receptionist can't avoid facing Muslim customers, and it might have helped if, in this case, the female companion were not dressed in a burka—the instant, loud announcer of religious membership. It reinforces the Hindu perception that Muslims are tenacious about their religion. The stereotype of a tough-minded community pops up. It is encircled by dire images of unseen men who don't mind blowing themselves up for the sake of killing others. If you have no friends in that community—it can't have ordinary men and women. The receptionist doesn't take long to decide that it's not worth taking a risk. He says 'no' although several rooms are vacant that evening. The man who had asked must wonder, and so does his wife, if they've been denied entry because they are Muslims. They know the truth but can't verify it. The silent cycle of distance, suspicion, dislike, fear and alienation rolls on.

It is an ominous cycle. The Muslim mind is by now fully used to living in that cycle, going through mood changes, and alternating currents of despair and resignation. In moments of total loss of hope for change, the mind surrenders to the spirit—of Islam. The mind tells the body not to worry. Any persecuted minority would face desperate moments by saying to itself: 'let them do what they wish'; 'I am who I am and shall not change'. A modern Muslim woman decides to wear a hijab. Now they may rape or kill me: I will face my destiny as a Muslim, not as a mere woman; only the police will say there was no evidence of communal intent. Over the last three decades, millions of Muslims have gone through this cycle and now they are reconciled to the new India over which they have no control. Within them, some clever men sell Muslim votes to the oppressors and gain a modicum of fame and power. Cities like Bhopal, Lucknow and Hyderabad have seen the rise and fall of many such barter-leaders in the Muslim community.

Ever since unified India broke up, the Muslim has been on bail. The desire to punish him is endemic. Even without Hindu nationalist victory in elections, the craving for revenge has been a popular trope. The word 'Pakistan' became a synonym for betrayal the day Partition took place. People who witnessed it and suffered had reason to feel that way, but the rest of India also toed the line crafted by generations of politicians. They kept the Partition alive by ensuring that Indians would learn nothing normal about their neighbours. Our media, cinema, schoolbooks, even literature kept the flame of blame burning, tacitly stoking the urge for revenge that finds satisfaction in small acts of disrespect and suspicion shown to a Muslim. It's like a cheap, permitted narcotic. Muslim children learn early that their teachers can't give them a fair deal. When they grow up, they are prepared, to live with a sense of risk all the time. They know that justice is not for them. Those who seek it shall suffer. It is the permanent, low-grade heat of half-violence.

Gandhi had imagined that he would dissolve the Hindu mind's Muslim complex. His benign attitude towards Muslims proved to be a terrible provocation for the venom stored up in several regions. Thickening this venom provided good employment to the organizational energies of Gandhi's enemies. They turned the venom into a vaccine—against sanity and peace—for future generations. It is injected at an early

age. Permanent prejudice works miracles; it packages hatred as
legitimate energy. Gandhi had become an object of hatred long
before he was killed. The hate-Gandhi industry had come into
motion almost as soon as he had started to acquire political
stature after returning from South Africa. At the heart of the
hate mission was Gandhi's message, that Hindus and Muslims
were essentially one, that true faith in God's authority can
never create gaps between human beings. Although a devout
Vaishnav Hindu himself, he publicly sought inspiration from
Jesus Christ, and his personal daily life included features of
Lord Mahavir's philosophy popularly known as Jainism. But the
purity of his conduct served no practical purpose. His detractors
remained resolute in staying clear of his ideas, especially the idea
of bringing Hinduism and Islam closer, relieving the burden
of antipathy towards Muslims weighing on the upper-caste
Hindu public mind. Muslim society and some of its tall leaders
played into the anything-but-Gandhi agenda. The common
Muslim paid a heavy price, and so did the nation as a whole, for
ignoring Gandhi's mission and hope.

His choice of non-violence as one of the two foundation
stones of his creed seems like a personal choice. It was made in
the face of the considerable weight of evidence that suggested
the necessity of violence for success in political conflict. More
than half the world was under colonial rule. It is hard to say
how wide Gandhi's awareness in his youth was about Europe's
colonizing powers although he knew about colonial rule outside
India. His life and struggle in South Africa indicate that his
concerns were focused on Indians although he had friends
among people of many different backgrounds. That many
fighters for India's freedom at that time were committed to
violent methods is well documented. Gandhi's awareness of
these fighters and their methods is copiously reflected in *Hind
Swaraj*. In this book, his rejection of violent aggression comes

across as a matter of logic, not emotion. But it seems wrong to claim that there was no emotion in his commitment to non-violence. How can a political choice sustained for so long be without emotion?

Naming the emotion would be hard. In the case of a commitment to violence, it is easy to name the emotion that sustains the commitment. It is hate. It has no contestants. In personal life too, hate serves better than any other emotion to consistently oppose someone we are angry with. If a justification is needed for staying opposed to a person, hate provides plenty. In personal life, hate permits you to entertain images of physical aggression and violence even if you cannot translate them into reality. These images provide a special kind of solace to the mind, especially when it is tired of feeling helpless and is close to risking hopelessness. Hate does not ask you nagging questions about good vs bad. Both sides can benefit from hate in a personal conflict. Things can, of course, get out of hand if the images invoked by hate end up playing an enabling role in a moment of opportunity. Hate can have a blinding effect in such moments, and the consequences will be tough.

In a collective or social conflict, hate plays a similar role. The big difference is that hate combined with power can have disastrous consequences as the history of Nazi Germany shows. But hate without power can also have terrible outcomes once violence breaks out. This is what happened in the Partition. These historical instances indicate how dangerous hate can be as an emotion sustained for long. Its solace-giving effect weakens with time because stored-up hate makes control of anger increasingly difficult. This may be the reason why Gandhi kept insisting on loving an enemy, an idea that must be among his least appreciated demands from people who otherwise respected him for his political stature and work. Gandhi's advice in this matter was undoubtedly rooted in

Christianity. Had Gandhi not been impressed with the Sermon
on the Mount and with Tolstoy, he might not have insisted on
enemy-love as a worthwhile accompaniment to politics against
a collective enemy.

It seems highly plausible that the Christian roots of
Gandhi's advocacy of love for one's enemy in a collective sense
made his appeal less convincing to a lot of people in certain
regions where the history of resistance was inseparable from
aggressive violence. Punjab was one such region. Its greatest
martyr Bhagat Singh had far greater appeal than Gandhi at the
time the British hung him. This has not changed with time.
Time has, however, wrought a miracle that only time can. It
has created an amalgam of Bhagat Singh's emotional resolve to
win and Gandhi's determination to remain non-violent to win.

This amalgam offers deeper insight into what
led the farmers to prevail in the only mass
movement the Hindu right has had to face
so far. The farmers who stayed for weeks
in the bitter cold of Delhi at the city's
border knew that their preparedness to face
violence would not lead their movement to
victory. Their leaders asked them to maintain
vigil against mischief, implying that the
formidable adversary would prefer some
violence. One leader pleaded for meekness,
asking potential mischief makers to 'take
pity on us'. Such a plea would seem quite
alien to Punjab's spirit and history; only
as a political choice, it made eminent sense.
We would not be wrong to attribute this
choice to Gandhi's invisible spirit and its
lasting influence. As for Bhagat Singh, his

living legacy was further sharpened by the physical presence of his niece at one of the protest sites. His nephew addressed a press conference during the protest. Hundreds of young people wore T-shirts carrying the familiar face of Bhagat Singh. Slogans were raised in his memory. He gave farmers the energy to sustain while Gandhi shaped their politics. Not merely the strategy of non-violence, their opposition to the corporate takeover and hostility to a government which had lent its full power and authority to facilitate it was also reminiscent of Gandhi's vision of an assertive rural India. In this historic struggle of Indian farmers for justice, the two great fighters for India's freedom have come together to lend each other strength and stamina. Bhagat Singh's impeccable sense of history and the necessity to break the aggressive march of today's corporate capital into the Indian countryside has merged with Gandhi's awareness that undeserving and undiscerning wielders of State power cannot be conquered with violence. Historians will, of course, continue to take sides on the controversy over Bhagat Singh's death sentence and whether Gandhi's imperfect sympathy affected his persuasive capacity to get the sentence commuted.

From anyone keen on becoming a *satyagrahi*, Gandhi demanded the willingness to sacrifice the common pleasures of life. If the list of Gandhi's demands were to be revised and updated, then the addiction to new instruments of communication technology might well call for consideration. Their novelty has been forgotten because of their glamorous and astonishing convenience. In under two decades, we have got so used to them that it seems impossible to imagine how anyone could function without them. Such a question is no doubt related to the government's policies and promotional resolve. 'Digital India' is not merely a slogan; it encapsulates a vast array of strategies the government has adopted to bring every citizen and child under a digital regime. To what extent India has become more efficient as a result of these strategies is a question we must distinguish from the nature of instrumentality inherent in digital machines of communication and social interaction.

Any answer to the question of whether an updated list of attributes of a satyagrahi might include digital distancing will depend on our larger view of technology. A simple or quick answer will not do because Gandhi's own initial approach to technology gradually mutated into a moderately sceptical view. Also, his practical engagement with machines was different from his argument. Having criticized the railways quite bluntly in *Hind Swaraj*, he used the transport extensively for the advancement of his politics. Yet, it may be important to bring the new technology of communication into the ambit of satyagraha. One reason is that the new instruments of sociability are owned by global monopolies. The degree of monopolistic control we witness today in the sphere of digital communication is unprecedented in the history of ownership. There is another, more vital, reason why we need to contemplate the nature of sociability that the new instruments permit.

This reason lies in the powers they have endowed upon the State, to deny the citizen any privacy whatsoever. Citizens have all the rights, but they are now fully disempowered. Many years ago, a visitor from Canada gifted me two books, *The Bias of Communication* by Harold Innis and *The Real World of Technology* by Ursula Franklin. The authors are unknown in India. Innis was an unusual economist who tried to explain the history of wealth and power by looking at modes of communication. He noticed that every technology has its own bias. It reorganizes the relationship between space and time, thereby changing the State's character. In history, regimes that depended on space-controlling technologies of communication did poorly on time management, including public memory. On the other hand, regimes that were good at controlling time did poorly in handling space. The balance between the two is decisive in sustaining a State's capacity and nature. Between regimes that communicated through rock carvings and empires that sent decrees, a deep distinction can be made, separating their moral agenda and the treatment of human needs. Whether or not a technology has an inherent nature of its own is yet another debate-worthy subject. The view that technology is merely a medium and how it is used is a matter of human choice is quite common. Few scientists have engaged with this popular view as intensely as Ursula Franklin did. She was an eminent metallurgist and, at the same time, an engaged social thinker. She thought a technology fully immerses us, shaping not just the way we do things, but also the way we think and relate to each other. A dominant technology, by this logic, wouldn't let us think about it as a possible source of some of our greatest problems.

Speed is in the nature of digital communication. In his *Six Memos to the Next Millennium,* Italo Calvino had indicated the importance that quickness and lightness will have in the future we now find ourselves in. These two characteristics, Calvino perhaps hoped, might help us to gain the awareness we need to face the State with its sovereignty over the new digital tools.

In its war against common citizens, especially the ones who might resist the future planned by it, the State uses new tools with greater control over them. These tools require so light a touch—barely a fingertip tap on a smooth little glass frame—that no one can entertain evil thoughts about what's going on. It all looks convenient, colourful, even benign. While the master sits in California, it's all well everywhere else.

The slow-moving rural culture, with the rudimentary essentials of life, became associated with Gandhi's name. But he did not invent this vision; he spotted it in tradition and put it to a new, political use. The value system he used and modernized can still be witnessed in certain settings and contexts. For instance, when an irksome neighbour falls ill or meets with an accident, a few people ask if the family needs help. A similar customary value covers hospitality. Teachers ask children not to take advantage of an injured member of the rival team. Internationally maintained modern norms for warring nations have their origins in similar old ethics sustained by tradition in several cultures. Gandhi used this old value system to develop his ethic of non-violence in oppositional politics. It was rooted in the belief that an adversary has human instincts which can be activated by demonstration of self-inflicted suffering. Gandhi saw the protestor's willingness to endure physical discomfort as a means of awakening the adversary's saner instincts.

Would Gandhi have attained his stature in Stalin's Russia, in Leopold's Congo, or in Hitler's Germany? Not at all, wrote Ved Mehta, after posing the question. Mehta was obviously right. Gandhi's vision of non-violent resistance wouldn't have meant much to men like Hitler or Stalin. Gandhi would have met an early death in one of Stalin's purges. Writing about Martin Luther King's struggle against racism, Mehta wondered if the idea of Gandhi could be replicated in the US. Mehta found Gandhi's standards of ethical conduct far too high for emulation by others.

Mehta recalls a dialogue between Gandhi and Nehru during the non-cooperation movement of 1922. On hearing about a violent incident in the Chauri Chaura village of Uttar Pradesh, Gandhi decided to withdraw the first all-India movement he had led. Nehru asked him, 'Must we train the 300 and odd millions of India in the theory and practice of non-violent action before we (can) move forward?' Gandhi's reply was short and unequivocal: 'Yes'. Gandhi's rigour did mellow with age and experience, but some of his tall contemporaries remained sceptical of his strategy of mass mobilization.

There is no point denying the fortuitous nature of the circumstances that permitted Gandhi's political experiment to survive for so long. In South Africa, where he worked in his youth, he first used his legal acumen to represent the rights of a community. This effort grew into a full-blown struggle though the focus was still specific. Once Gandhi returned to India, the focus of his politics widened so rapidly that even he was taken by surprise. His philosophy let him assume that *all* human beings have a God-element: their conscience. In some, it gets clouded or pressed down, but it can be awakened. It follows that if a man chooses to accept the physical suffering that an oppressive opponent can inflict upon him, the opponent's conscience might get rekindled. Gandhi did not imagine that there could be humans without any God-element left in them. A Pol Pot was beyond Gandhi's imagination. The fact that he thought of writing a letter to Hitler suggests that he did not have an accurate understanding of the Nazi leader. One has the same feeling about his statement on what Jews and the victims of the atomic bomb in Hiroshima should have done.

Let me interject. I know what Munna is hinting at. Our present-day reality poses similar problems of disbelief. Is it possible, we

ask, that a district administrator and
his police counterpart decide to burn the
corpse of a raped girl in order to destroy
any evidence her body might have contained?
We too, like Gandhi, feel unprepared to
hear or imagine this. We don't like to
think that civil servants can be like that.
A shield of faith that Gandhi had smelted
himself protected him—from horrors that
might have been too much for him. Thích
Nhất Hạnh applies the Buddha's knowledge
to recommend a similar shield to us all,
without meaning to suggest that we should
keep ourselves in the dark.

Peaceful protest is the cliché we have inherited from Gandhi. It
is recognized as a democratic right in many countries, including
ours. However, in Gandhi's canon of non-violent warfare,
protest can't merely be a form of expression. One must ask:
'expression of what?' The answer will reveal whether the protest
is real and for a collective cause. It is an expression addressed to
those who hold power. It aims to arouse their conscience—their
deeper humanity. (It is assumed they have it.) By doing that, the
protestor takes a risk—of irritating the powerful. How much and
what kind of risk it is depends on who your protest is addressing
and the kind of power regime they run. There can be no general
theory of Gandhian protest. It demands adjustable intelligence
from the protestors—they must have the capacity to read the
regime's mind and know its habits. A blunt regime that has no
intellectual acumen may have little patience with a protest. It
may require protracted mollifying before its frozen conscience
can be aroused. Facing such a regime may incur dire risk—not
merely of a violent encounter, but of long-term cynicism among

the protestors. When Gandhi was in command, he acted like an artist, personalizing his method in ways no one else might be able to emulate. The use of self-inflicted physical suffering—in prolonged fasts—was quite often strategic. It bewildered the British and his Indian opponents alike. As a quasi-religious practice, fasting teased the flag-bearers of Hindu nationalism. His popularity among the masses demoralized them. They didn't know what to make of him and still don't, but they realize he is much too global to be condemned.

The phrase 'non-violent resistance' sounds strange, somewhat droll. Without its association with Gandhi, the idea would have little meaning or attraction left by now. He made it look credible. People exaggerate when they—especially, the writers of school history books and composers of film songs—say that Gandhi wrought a miracle with his weapons of non-violence. It's a grand oxymoron. The miracle myth is losing its gloss now. Despite all he managed to achieve, hardly anyone now believes that a serious conflict can be overcome without violence. India's new managers are keen to rewrite history to teach the young generation that attributing India's freedom to Gandhi's leadership is wrong. They are just as uncomfortable with Gandhi's other weapon: truth. Its day is over as well. Official statistics were its last bastion, and now they are fraught with controversies. When they don't strike a grand tune of achievement, they are held back, in deep cupboards. No one minds if the more conscientious officials step down. Truth wouldn't get you far in professional life. In politics, you'd be a laughing stock. Strategic lying, hiding facts, circulating false information are the toolkits of power. The public recognizes these toolkits and smiles when they are used.

Transposing him is entertaining and silly, but the Gandhi myth is so impelling. Some Gandhians say he would've been an avid user of social media today. Would he join e-protests?

The effort it takes is so miniscule, so a busy Gandhi wouldn't mind, they will argue. He is invoked to deal with a host of questions we can't handle without the fear of our progressive personalities being put under a cloud. Orwell wrongly denied Gandhi the label of humanism. He would certainly not have called him progressive. Gandhi would have condemned artificial intelligence and its products like facial recognition. We can't stretch Gandhi. He is no plastic figure. His metal or stone busts are mere selfie spots now. Words alone can protect him from predators.

III

Who can represent the city of Bhopal? The question need
not be confined just to Bhopal, though for me it is. Perhaps
we need to ask about every village and town because it is no
easy matter to represent others. My uncle was the king of
our state, but he hardly represented our town or the villages
around. Such a thought would have amused him. He was wise
enough to realize that he was far too wealthy and cultured to
represent the common folk. And yet, in an obvious sense, he
did represent them, and that is how, and why, the British dealt
with him. I am already getting confused between recognition
and representation. Someone who might represent others must
be at least a little bit like them. If they are mostly poor, he
can hardly be the owner of so much wealth that he can't figure
out how someone with limited means copes with life, his own
and his family's. Without something in common between
a representative and those he represents, there can hardly be
any substance to this idea. It is basic to democracy—*because*
representation also brings the status of a leader. Not everyone
can be allowed to lead. If this were not so, then a person who

arouses a mob and drives it to a frenzy would also qualify to be a leader. Many such 'leaders' emerged in cities across northern India when Indira Gandhi was assassinated. And mob leaders had had a great time when the Partition loomed on the horizon of freedom.

How Bhopal has arrived where it is, is a forked, tortuous story. It started with two bold dreams. After the dreams were stretched into reality, there came a terrifying moment in the first dream. The other one is dragging on, like a Bollywood movie that started well but lost track. In between the two dreams lay the story of an uneasy, deluded city, Bhopal. I have now figured out the allegory hidden in that story. I am no more surprised that the majority of its voting citizenry didn't mind being told that Gandhi's assassin was a patriot. The candidate who said so publicly won the city's seat in the Parliament. A Hindi poet who loves Bhopal publicly expressed his anxiety over the prospect of the city being represented by someone parachuted there. He saw it as a cynical election ploy that might threaten the city's reputation. I don't know how he felt when the parachuted nominee was declared victorious with a huge margin of votes.

I felt sick that evening. The counting of votes had indicated the trend by the afternoon, but I didn't want to believe it. Doctors say that it is not good for your blood pressure if you hold back a gnawing thought. When it was no longer possible to hold it back, the thought overwhelmed me. I felt angry, cheated, sorry—for myself, for I had once risked my life for Bhopal. How could that city now hit me so hard when I was old and too frail to sustain the blow? In my fury, I forgot that a city has no mind or motive. From anger to sudden grief, then a pause to regain conscious, sensible balance; a second wave of disbelief at what had happened pushed me towards the fear that this was just the beginning of the loss of India itself. It

all happened quickly, wrenching me towards a stroke. Days
later, after medical help and rest, I still felt possessed, unable
to return to reality from old images and memories—of the big
lake shining eternally in moonlight, for that is how I had seen
it first, long ago.

It was bigger than the city then, hemming it from the
west, spread out below the gentle Shymala Hill. Together they
symbolized Bhopal. They caused an evening breeze to rise, so
the residents would feel comforted all year round. But how
could I lump all residents into one? There were two kinds. The
old Bhopalis were different; one could tell them by their accent
and demeanour. The new arrivals conjured up a fresh city for
themselves—with a new market, a legislature, a tall secretariat,
and a sprawling colony of white and beige bungalows. The
old city did not die, but it couldn't grow either, not in its own
style, anyway. Among the newly arrived were the *sahibs* and
the people's representatives who had the power to decide what
would happen next. They ordered a star-shaped miracle factory
to be raised in the eastern corner. It made Bhopal an icon of
India's industrial ambitions, to use advanced chemistry to
transform old-style farming. Their axiomatic slogan was rural
development. It covered the backyard of every city, the rural
hinterland of the entire nation. Old Bhopal was allowed to
carry on its pre-industrial pursuits like stitching velvet pouches.

My father bought me one when I travelled with him to
Bhopal as a boy. Its velvet was dark maroon. The shiny silver
hemming made it look grand. It had two strings sown across
the opening. If you pulled the strings tight, the pouch squeezed
itself like a tiny, live pet. What could I possibly use this pouch
for, I wondered. As a small boy, I loved being allowed to chew
a paan because it was forbidden. An old woman who attended
to my mother secretly gave me a part of a paan now and then.
Using my little pouch to keep a paan was a scintillating fantasy

I travelled with. Back home, my first thought was to find out how K. might look at the maroon object. I could see a jealous gleam in his eyes as he fingered the velvet. Then he asked the question I had asked myself:

'What will you do with it?'

I might have said 'coins' or something like that when K. said: 'Give it to your mother—for paans.'

'She already has two,' I was quick to point out . . .

'Both look shabby . . . One is torn.'

'Shabby? Did you say shabby?'

That word upset me so fast and so thoroughly that I found myself ready, in a split second, to push K. down. If I didn't, the reason must be the big parrot. Where we stood was a few steps away from his brass cage. It was shining in the golden shaft of the winter sun. Had I punched K., the parrot would have shrieked. K. was lean and shorter. He had sensed my anger—and he knew exactly what had caused it—the adjective he had used for my mother's paan purses. For me, they had a pleasant scent from daily use: of beetle nut and lime. It was an enticing mix. And K. was upset that he had said something stupid. I knew my mother was so fond of him that she handed him a paan when I wasn't around and watching. The paan prohibition applied more strictly to me. My pouch remained empty, shiny, precious, till I lost and forgot it—in what order I don't care to remember. But Bhopal stayed fresh and beautiful.

It survived its apocalypse that nearly killed me with secondary exposure, while I was giving handouts to the victims. I was sure Bhopal would flourish again, rising from the ashes and that sort of thing. With its reputation as an arts centre growing, riding the waves of Kumar Gandharva's *taans*, Bhopal could conquer its misfortune. Success and vicinity to power makes you giddy. I was like that, not ready to accept that Bhopal was poisoned so thoroughly that the poison in it would now breed its own varieties, and they would mutate further, saturating the unfortunate city in ways more numerous than civil servants and their political masters would know how to count. The poison silently spread through the veins of the new colonies—the smooth slopes, the nearby sub-colonies where the sahibs' servants lived, the far-off slums where the countless migrants from villages lived with their cows, goats and rats. By demolition time, eight years later in distant Ayodhya, poison was everywhere. And yet, I was oblivious: happy to state that Bhopal would soon be an education hub; meaning coaching, but I didn't mind or clarify, even to myself. K. used to get upset with me in those days. His ideas about education were purer, out of sync with new trends. He stays aloof—doesn't follow trends.

I have taken a long time to emulate K.'s stance, and I am not there yet. His ability to maintain psychological distance from things he doesn't like has bothered me throughout our adult lives. Whenever I appreciate it, he thinks I am poking fun. He says he envies me—my sensibility. He must be ironical; in any case, he is so much wiser—no mixing of emotions with thoughts, even memories, even the charming ones. How can I say that K. is not bothered about India's future? Perhaps his mother gave him practical wisdom. I know she loved me as much if not more than him. At times, his equanimity bothers me. If only I could drive him a bit crazy about something— anything, I would feel more reassured about *his* future. After retirement, he looks so conveniently fed up, with everything. India is too amorphous for him to relate to, he says. If it is going to ruin itself, so be it, he says. When I object, he throws the Dalai Lama at me. Apparently, the Buddhist teacher has said that anxiety is pointless. If you can do something, do it; if you can't, why worry? I wish I could benefit from that. When you get into civil service, the idea that you can do something about everything is drilled into you. You become a permanent patriot. I did all I could to help the dying and the injured in Bhopal, but now I must reconcile to its fate. It's hard.

My current despair had set in weeks before the 2019 election, but I had not lost all hope of the Hindu nationalists losing. Several old friends who live in Bhopal were convinced that the Congress candidate, a former chief minister, would win. He was no angel, and no native of Bhopal either, but he offered himself to carry a deadly burden. The news of his defeat shouldn't have shocked me, but his rival's victory got to me. I'd thought Bhopal wouldn't vote for someone who had publicly said that Godse was a patriot. Such an endorsement of Gandhi's assassin, I had assumed, would repel the public of the city I'd come to regard as mine. The election result came like the news of a personal disaster, like the collapse of the last standing wall of a castle.

My doctor friend Ravi, who had looked after me that night, was convinced that though I had suffered a minor stroke, it had left no trace as such. But, I had continued to feel off balance. The shock of the election outcome in Bhopal had not worn off. The initial tremor gone, the feeling of being a stranger had set in. Bhopal, the city I had served in its hour of horror, had now become a blank space on India's map. No matter how hard I tried, I could not recall anything or anyone from the years I had spent in various positions in Vallabh Bhawan, the secretariat. Was I losing my memory? The question filled me with fear and apprehension.

When Gandhi was still around and enjoyed unmatched stature among political leaders, many resented his politics and hated him personally. Many held him directly responsible for the division of India into two nation-states. Others thought he could have prevented it. Their negative feelings towards him have lived on and spread over the years. Nowadays, it is fashionable to say that India would have been better off without

Gandhi. He was aware of such views when his life was close to its end. We hardly need evidence to say that Gandhi was afflicted by a deep sense of failure in the chief mission of his life—unity among the people of India. In its palpable absence, Gandhi felt helpless in the face of India's impending Partition. He knew he couldn't prevent it, but more than Partition, the daily violence and religious hatred hit him hard.

Though he had chased India's freedom as his goal for nearly half his life, on the first day of freedom he chose to stay away from the site of celebratory joy—New Delhi. He must have felt sick with sorrow. He preferred to be among riotous mobs in faraway Bengal where the remnants of his dream were being shredded. He was determined—not to feel scared of raw blood; and he had seen enough of hatred. It is a stupid belief we maintain that everybody loved him because he loved everyone. Such a treacle is common. Gandhi must have gleaned from Christ's life that practicing love is a dangerous business. Already in the 1930s, Gandhi had tasted social distancing. It proved a long decade, after a spectacular start with salt. He tried changing his focus—from salt to soil, so to say. Instead of freedom and its politics, he took shelter in village work. It was too late for such a diversion to help. Hatred was sprouting across the northern plains. Surrendering to it was not an option, so when the British announced their decision to give India smudgy freedom, Gandhi had no choices left.

He physically intervened, using his frail body to hold riot-ready souls apart from each other. His old, steely will was there to compensate for the loss of strength and despair. But neither his resolve nor his courage sufficed to avoid the recognition of failure in the end. Different kinds of historical evidence exist to indicate that Gandhi took Partition and the riots accompanying it as an acknowledgement of his inadequacy. He couldn't deliver a single, free India to Indians. It sounds mad that someone had aspired to take on such a responsibility. Biographers and psychologists have suggested feelings of intense loneliness, yearning for maternal care and closure to life as constituents of Gandhi's mood between August 1947 and January of the new year. If he wanted to die for us, he did.

That Indians of all faiths had trusted him, and he had failed to deliver his promise is not far from the truth he might have sensed. It was that kind of relationship: he knew what the millions were thinking. Seven decades on, one can see the facets of the relationship: Gandhi enjoys both veneration and dislike. Many hate him as if he were still alive. They believe he was wrong from the start. In the end, they think what K. and I as two adolescents had once thought. Our model was chemistry. My Grade 10 teacher at Scindia had explained that if the two elements that form a compound are separated, they would continue to enjoy independent existence. I can't recall how that idea mutated in my juvenile intellect. That summer, when I met K., I applied my chemical knowledge to ask him why Hindus can't have India for themselves when Muslims have chosen to separate. I was pleased when K. seemed impressed. It was our first jointly sculpted political theory. Neither of us wanted to share it with anyone—certainly not with K.'s mother. This was not the only secret between us, but it was special. Somehow we knew its explosive implications: it might trigger a riot if we were not careful. Two boys on the mount, we enjoyed the view and our pact.

We discarded our theory when we forgot it. Other exciting subjects took over our holiday meetings and letters. I don't remember when—it hardly matters. What matters is that a great number of people had a similar theory and that they never abandoned it? They tailored a sumptuous ideology out of it. They used it to trigger riots, win elections, gain clout—in municipal wards, and in provincial caves of legitimate power before finally conquering the nation that Muslims had once conquered. It brought them great satisfaction, but new heights were waiting to be scaled. The fiery flag, the watery flower worked wonders and horrors. They can now openly criticize Gandhi, praise his assassin, and tell Muslims to go home. And not just Muslims. Anyone who cheers when the Pakistani cricket team wins can also leave. India's teen age has arrived.

It was all Gandhi's doing, they say. If you go by What'sApp, there is more hate for Gandhi now than love. Digital dialogue about him is more popular among his detractors; for others, he is a bit too arcane to claim, let alone politically utilize, although the solemnity of special occasions is always maintained. Hindu nationalists have completed their translation of Gandhi. He is the anointed philosopher of *their* Clean India mission. The rest of him is merchandise for souvenir shops, one for each of the hundreds of tourist sites they are nurturing. Their hatred gives them both energy and motivation. It comfortably hides their envy, for Gandhi still being so much taller than their leaders. Gandhi knew his people well, that they would turn him into another idol to worship. He had singled himself out for far too long, and idolizing had already emerged, exactly as Tagore had warned. People who feel that in being an architect of his failure, he harmed India by assuming the role of its highest leader can claim a certain logical accuracy in their thought. This logic helps them feel free of guilt for his violent death which gives some relief and satisfaction too. These feelings are but a step away from gratitude to his murderer. That Gandhi was worth being killed at such an advanced age itself speaks of his significance for his haters.

With the passage of time, it was expected that his aura would fade, and his presence subside. To an extent, this did happen, but his stamp on the collective psyche has remained intact, perhaps because children hear about him in considerable

detail and with emotion when they are very young. Something
of that emotional appeal remains when they grow up. This may
be one reason why Gandhi's detractors failed, till quite recently,
in changing the public perception of Gandhi by any significant
measure. Their attempts to discredit him achieved success
within the ideological circles of Hindu nationalist politics.
How far their propaganda against Gandhi had come became
apparent in Bhopal in the summer of 2019.

Bhopal was special for me for many reasons. I had spent a
considerable part of my career there. I liked it as a city. Some
of my close friends still live there. I was in Bhopal when the
gas catastrophe struck the city in the winter of 1984. The gas
tragedy gave Bhopal the kind of fame no city would ever want
to have. The poisonous gas spewing out of a leaky cylinder
of the Union Carbide factory killed an uncounted number of
people in one night. Over the following days, weeks, months
and years, people kept dying. It was like war without a war.
One felt confused and aghast. You didn't want to think about
your friends and others you knew in the city. Nor did you know
how to think of the masses who faced the gas in their beds, ran
out and collapsed. As the first week passed and fresh news of
deaths and terrible lung injuries kept coming, one felt despair
about the future of a beautiful city. Thirty-six years later, the
exact number of the dead continues to be debated, and the
number of those injured as a result of inhaling the poisonous
air is estimated to be in the hundreds of thousands. Dying on
account of gas-related causes has been everyday news for so
long that it arouses no interest. Some of the officers who were
in charge of handling the tragedy have died over the years due
to reasons that remain medically controversial.

Innocence also calls for ignorance, and for a long time, I did
not know that old Bhopal was largely Muslim, that my little
velvet pouch was part of a Muslim heritage. The transformation

of the old city into a chaotic, poverty-stricken ghetto occurred long after Bhopal became the capital of Madhya Pradesh in 1956. To say that is a bit incorrect. Bhopal didn't 'become' the capital of Madhya Pradesh: Nehru wanted it, otherwise, the prestige would have gone to Jabalpur. Nehru must have thought that Muslim-dominated Bhopal would promote India's secular credentials. He believed in such benign tricks, and they did work for quite a while. What struck Bhopal twenty-eight years after its elevation was no doubt a secular accident, but the majority of the poor who died in it were most probably Muslim—though, of course, there is no such communal count.

But Bhopal's story didn't have to be that way. Nothing was inevitable, but after a while things fell into a pattern and the outcome now looks to have been the only likelihood. Two parallel destinies of the city have been taking shape since the mid-1970s. One was aesthetic, the other was industrial. Bharat Bhawan, a national centre of the arts, and Union Carbide, a multinational pesticide factory were competing to bend Bhopal's story. The city had a long tradition of music and design. The new institution would bring artistes from all over India and overseas, making the city a crucible of creative urge, with long tunnel galleries dug into the ground and roof-top theatres. Its sunken architecture would offset the tall metallic pipes and chimneys of the gigantic pesticide factory—the star-shaped symbol of India's tryst with chemical, magical engineering, the transformer of village life, food shortages, and of low-yielding crops.

I was in Bhopal during the Emergency. I knew the city well, but this time I was struck by how different it felt from the rest of Madhya Pradesh, especially from the regions I had known as a boy and as a young recruit to the civil service. My posting this time was in a new institution, born in a senior, visionary civil servant's mind. The chief minister was keen that the new institution, an ambitious centre for the arts and culture, should be inaugurated as quickly as possible by Indira Gandhi. She was the official empress of India at the time and the entire bureaucracy was eager to appear optimistic about the success of her Emergency mission to cleanse the old country of all its evils and blemishes with her 20-Point Programme. The greasiest blemish was the opposition led by the ageing Gandhian leader from Bihar, Jayaprakash Narayan.

Equipped with a fancy centre of modern arts, Bhopal would symbolize a new, bold India—with an atom bomb and regional clout displayed by dismembering Pakistan. As for the real city, no one had time to spot the early signs of religious separation that had set in following the crushing defeat of Pakistan in the war of 1971. The creation of Bangladesh had stunned the Muslim community across India. A new chapter of regional history had begun when Pakistan broke, and its western lump skidded towards the harder Middle Eastern Islam.

Long before Independence and Partition, Bhopal was ruled by three Muslim women. These Begums are still famous for the good, modern things they did, like starting schools for girls. That history does not matter now. In today's Bhopal, as in the rest of India, denial of any role to Muslims in nation-building is in fashion. The object is to make Muslims feel unvalued, and dependent on the mercy of the majority. In Bhopal's new ethos, no Muslim can relax.

Bhopal is not Gujarat, yet, but it has mutated. Its distinctive culture is now a memory. My old friend Manzoor Ahtesham captured the change in his book, *Sookha Bargad* (Dried-Up Banyan). It dates the city's internal partition to the mid-1960s. The father figure in the story, an elderly lawyer, lives on under the benign Nehruvian promise that Partition would make no difference to India. Well, it did, and Bhopal witnessed incremental fragmentation. The two wars with Pakistan—the second one leading to its breakup—and the Middle Eastern money pipeline and the gradual build-up of Hindu separatism sapped the old banyan bit by bit. It is a sad story, yet it leaves us with Rashida, the lawyer's feisty daughter who turns down a proposal for marriage to a wealthy family in Pakistan.

But Bhopal was no longer Rashida's alone. The new, sprawling Bhopal, the city of government servants, all but swallowed the old town. The *burra* sahibs' bungalows, the clerks' quarters, and the swarming migrants from the hinterland pushed aside Muslim Bhopal. Its unique language could still be heard, but All India Radio and television had no use for it. In normal towns of British India, the civil servants and the judges and the doctors lived on the outskirts in their civil lines; but Bhopal was now civil lines all over. The yellow bungalows and quarters dotting the gentle, rolling slopes symbolized the special breed of democracy where the bureaucracy was in charge of the people, equipping them with relevant dreams and procedures to fulfil them. The climate was perfect: gentle winters, and summers moderated by a vast and beautiful lake. No one could imagine such a nice place would see people inhaling airborne poison and collapsing in their thousands overnight and for years to come.

Bharat Bhawan, the elegant centre for the arts boosted my affection for the city. For a brief period, Bhopal's new identity, as a patron of theatre, dance, music, painting and crafts, blossomed. No other city in India received the kind of public financial investment that Bhopal got for promoting creative expression. Bharat Bhawan was unique. Instead of a majestic structure visible from a distance, Bharat Bhawan was a sunken building, entirely below the ground level, designed like an intricate web of galleries, halls and workspaces spread across what would have been the basement of a normal building. You descend into a modern range of cavernous spaces. As a government building, it was a spectacular departure from what the Public Works Department had been relentlessly churning out since the nineteenth century. Bharat Bhawan was a statement of freedom, to design modernity afresh.

What Bhopal went through on the night of 4 December 1984 was something like a chemical bombing. The news of Indira Gandhi's assassination had come just over a month earlier. The anti-Sikh riots it had triggered in many cities, including Bhopal, had not yet subsided when the gas disaster struck. Was it an uncanny coincidence? The pain that Bhopal suffered and endured had no precedence in India's industrial history and few parallels in the world. After the initial shock of the reality of the disaster, the city did recover, painfully slowly and without doing justice to the vast numbers of the poor and others suffering the long-term, gradually unfolding consequences of the poisonous gas. Some 4000 people are believed to have died within minutes after the gas started leaking—or so says the official undercount. Another 14000 died over the following weeks. Gradually, the rate of death declined, but every now and then one continued to learn what it meant to live with compromised lungs. (*A report on coronavirus deaths that came two years after Munna's death said that 73 per cent of the fatalities in Bhopal were of people affected by the 1984 gas emission—K.*). There are still many others who had escaped instant death after the gas leak and also in the years that followed but carried on suffering from weakened lungs and pain. As a parallel process, their search for justice through the courts, from Bhopal to Delhi to New York, brought more pain. The city that had dreamt of becoming a centre for the pursuit of aesthetic sensibility and urban beauty became a city of pain and the desire to conceal it.

The pesticide factory had commenced operations in 1969. The late 1960s were years of radical transition in India's agricultural economy. Its modernization meant the promotion of high-yielding varieties of crops along with the use of chemical fertilizers and pesticides. Official knowledge asks us to believe that Bhopal was chosen as an appropriate site for a pesticide factory because the city was centrally located and well-connected. Another reason must be the attractions that a newly formed and industrially backward state presented to investors. They needed incentives to come into such regions and hefty incentives they received in states like MP. The Green Revolution was looming on the horizon. An agro-industrial market was going to emerge, featuring new varieties of seeds, chemical fertilizers and pesticides. The colour green now symbolizes purified air, water and soil; in the Green Revolution of the late 1960s, green implied higher yields by extermination of weeds, pests and insects.

The great pest killer DDT—it fetched a Nobel prize for its inventor—was already being produced since 1954 by Hindustan Insecticide Limited. It was an insect killer, but its lore raced across the nation as a malaria controller. Rachel Carson's revelations in *Silent Spring* took a while to reach us. She proved that DDT was a slow-speed, cancer-causing poison. Cost-benefit analysis never fails to permit such poisons to remain in the market, so DDT still sells and kills, in devious, dexterous style. Union Carbide's new product, Sevin, is more effective and reaches out to a far greater variety of plant killers—close to a million perhaps. You need very advanced chemistry to make sense of its insecticidal capacity. Its white crystalline powder is said to be safe for human health. Nevertheless, professors of agriculture ask farmers to put on gloves and masks before spraying any pest killer, but farmers don't listen. In Punjab, where modern farming methods took hold before anywhere else, farmers travel to Bikaner in Rajasthan to seek cancer treatment at a cutting-edge hospital. They catch the so-called 'cancer train' at Bhatinda. Many among them now know what caused their cancer, but pesticides are well entrenched, like big dams. Both are symbols of modernization.

Two women challenged the State's choice of India's route to modernity. In them, you see not just traces of Gandhi, but his ongoing struggle. What the Narmada River was for Medha Patkar, indigenous grains were for Vandana Shiva. They have spent a life in opposition, spent on the margins. Medha Patkar chose dams as her site of a life-long struggle. She was arrested several times. Holding her in police custody was no small task. Different officers handled it each time. Once it was my turn. She looked so frail and straightforward, resolute and articulate, I thought I was fortunate to have a glimpse of a bit of Gandhi. The giant dam she was blocking on the Narmada has recently been inaugurated. A short while later, a towering, metal statue of Patel was unveiled. Hotels with colourful buntings and pleasure boats will be next. Parts of a village continue to shimmer from its watery grave. The project was successful, but the bipolar gap between Patkar and the State proved unbridgeable. The same thing happened over Vandana Shiva's stand against high-yielding, pesticide-dependent crops. After the Bhopal catastrophe, one hoped that the chemical lobby might slow down. It was silly to expect that. Vandana Shiva showed how the Green Revolution was not the only way India might have become self-sufficient.

Secular nationalists like me think that Hindutva alone can destroy India. We ignore other ways that harm the old country. The ideology of developmentalism is now endorsed with matching enthusiasm by the secular and the Hindu nationalists. There is just one difference left between the two camps: the Hindu guys maintain a Swadeshi brigade. No one now notices its lame-duck character. Brigade members themselves don't mind; they are integral to the great family of Hindu, indigenous nationalism. It has multiple tongues, variegated muscles. The

Swadeshi chant calms the public nerve, reassuring the impatient. It also signals to the naïve among Gandhi's leftovers that the slogan—it was not *his* invention—has relevance. And Khadi is the other great banner. It placates Gandhi's ghost, transmuting his fight into a hand-made gift for the festive season.

Religious nationalism has adopted warmongering as its natural, permanent activity. It calls for building India's military might so that Hindu pride can hold the world in awe. Weapon-manufacturing will now be our industrial priority, and soon enough we will become an arms-exporting nation. That is the role assigned to science. It was already playing that role for a while, but there was some room for other things, like education and research. They have been outsourced. Swaraj is now absorbed within the State's violent capacities. You can't beat the clarity of the current picture and plan. If anyone had any doubt, it can now be shed—that Gandhi was suspicious of modern science. It would take humanity towards self-destruction. Somehow he hoped that India could be stopped from going the West's scientific way to perdition. I don't know why Godse didn't charge Gandhi for being anti-science. The trial court had given him free rein to present his encompassing list of charges against the man he had shot. Had he read Gandhi, he might well have included Gandhi's 'unscientific' temper in his litany of complaints. Surely it constituted a threat to the nation's progress. But Godse might have had other reasons for ignoring this aspect of Gandhi. Godse's ideological mentors and mates held Western science and its technological achievements—especially in weaponry—in awe. All they wanted, and still do, is an acknowledgement that stem cell grafting was performed in ancient India. It hurts them that India is considered backwards in modern science while just about every modern invention and theory is already mentioned in the Vedas.

If you have no time to think about it, you will find Gandhi anti-science. Nothing could be farther from the truth. I am not talking about historical facts, speeches, correspondence, etc. If these were sufficient to grasp Gandhi, even Savarkar and Godse would have grasped him. All three, I mean Gandhi, Savarkar and Godse, lived in times when science meant miracles. From railways and light bulbs to motor cars, science had already become a byword for amazement before the twentieth century began. That association with science never weakened in the colonized mind. The Wright brothers' flying machine did the rest: from then onwards science would mean miracles. That idea never died. I crammed a good-length essay on 'Miracles of Science' for my matriculate boards. The other colonial theory was that science is power. According to it, guns, bombs and grenades are the West's source of dominance. Gandhi accepted that brute force helped the West to conquer India, but that is not the crux of his argument and historical sense. His point is that India lost because it had no inner strength left. This idea freed Gandhi from the common nationalist stereotype of science as a miracle and the core of Western power.

He drew a bigger picture. The books he read convinced him that there were two views one could take on science: the mesmerized admirer's view, and the critical view. He took the latter. He was unhappy that a scientist's mind had no room for moral considerations, that even Einstein couldn't stop the use of his science to kill millions. Gandhi's science is different. It ignores nothing and worries about everything. It rejects the common distinction between man-made and natural disasters. He does not separate the human from the non-human world. The idea has radical implications. If man is nature, we can't look upon its occasional impact on mankind as a one-sided matter. Both our physical and psychological lives are dependent on nature. Throughout his life, Gandhi used nature as his guide and main resource for health.

In this role, 'nature' meant one's body—with its own will to function well, guided by a purposive mind. This is Gandhi's science. It is excessive, just like Hiroshima and Bhopal science. The narratives of self-curing and stopping others from medical help read like suspense stories where patient suffering blossoms in full cure. Call it personal science, but actually, it's like a farmer's knowledge, born in experience and quiet awareness. Agricultural universities ignored it and promoted advanced chemicals. A few decades later one heard about rural suicides. (In one of my in-service trainings, I was told about Durkheim and his sociology of suicide; he thought it was an urban thing). Not one, two or even a few, but hundreds of thousands killed themselves, first in Maharashtra, and then it spread. A little dose of pesticide proved efficacious for self-annihilation. Social scientists—faithful siblings of science—found debt burden to be a common cause. The national Bhopal project was acquitted.

Huxley saw in Gandhi a way out of the impending brave new world. It would boldly control all men and women, their bodies and thoughts. It would be new in its dismissal of the human right to freedom. It was a cold prognosis. When it was published, it seemed distant. It's no longer science fiction. Digital control and collaboration between the State and financial conglomerates have brought the world close to Huxley's portrait. And now, we are told that climate change can be reversed if we cooperate. States and companies are working hard together to slow down global warming. Huxley was unhappy as Gandhi received a State funeral—with cannon salutes and warplanes. He escaped co-option in life, but death proved harder. Gandhi asks us to go to the bottom in order to locate the truth. The factory that killed tens of thousands—and more are still dying from residual effects—was part of a killer project. This is Gandhi's unhesitating science—not a handmaiden of governments and corporate monopolies. Gandhi's science invites us to make connections. The ones he draws are not wild; just wide enough to overcome orthodoxies.

Just as there is no sense in separating man-made and natural disasters, there is no basis to put the living and the non-living in two rival categories. This denial carries no copyright symbol, and Gandhi's biographers have traced it to the influence of Jainism. According to Jain philosophy, that which seems non-living today will live one day, like a stone eventually degrading into fertile soil—with micro-organisms that will tempt agriculture scientists to reach out for a measure of approved poison. Forget about its source, such ideas are common among the rural masses. They believe rivers to be alive, and not because they flow. River worship extends to ponds, big and small. All that Gandhi did was to assemble and wrap up folk beliefs into a long hand-written letter to be read by future generations when they have time and feel terrified by humanity's impending death. Reading this letter has sustained me over the months that have passed since the Bhopal election. I had forgotten him, but Gandhi was there. Like a farmer, he spread seeds across our land. Some fell in my primary school. I had nearly lost them, like millions of others. I am lucky that the seeds didn't die. They sprouted when the dark surrounded me.

The nation he gifted us was for all. That's why he is called father. The neo-nationalists can't understand why Gandhi is so hard to finish off. The seeds he sowed are far too many to dig out and destroy. To destroy them all would require the soil itself to be changed. That's the kind of project Bhopal needed because the groundwater around the factory had absorbed the lethal chemicals. They are gradually spreading, in the soil.

The moral bond between mankind and nature has broken down. Slow disasters are happening all the time, and occasionally you face a dramatic disaster like Bhopal. A moral bond works when the two sides are equal. If one has conquered the other—and feels proud of it—the bond has no value left in it. Mankind's conquest over nature is a celebrated achievement of science. There are no signs of any regret over it; in fact, the determination to stamp out any retaliation on nature's part is as strong as ever, despite the rhetoric of environmental concerns. The moment bird flu infects a few humans, millions of birds are killed to stop the spread of the virus. Chemical fertilizers, pesticides and the so-called Green Revolution were justified by reference to a fungal infection that destroyed crops and made India food-dependent. The Bhopal factory was the culmination of this chain of arguments.

Generations of the educated middle class have been coached to view Gandhi's perception of science as one of the many fatherly eccentricities of Gandhi. For them, Nehru compensates for Gandhi on this question of science. In any case, both enjoy life at the margin these days. To sort out their dialogue over India's progress would be tedious—and pointless as well. Nehru did recognize the 'disease of gigantism' when he saw how big dams eat up resources and livelihoods. Gandhi was choosy about science and technology for reasons that humanity now finds glowering everywhere. The Singer sewing machine was his model; it chewed up no one's income.

To the Hindu nationalists, Gandhi's fatherly foibles pose no problem as such, but the status poses a dilemma they can't resolve. They revere Subhash Chandra Bose, and it is he who addressed Gandhi as the father of the nation. The nation Bose was referring to was like Gandhi himself—open to all faiths: giving not just equal respect to all religions but believing in all of them because they are all equally true. That kind of nation contrasts with the neo-nationalists' notion of India and their understanding of Hinduism itself. Theirs is a territorial, narrow version of the ancient faith. Gandhi practised it by being Gandhi. He became a metaphor for the nation that Subhash Chandra Bose identified with. That's the reason he gave Gandhi a father's status. Tied up in knots as they are, the Hindu nationalists can't appreciate this title though they love Bose.

Their rejection of Gandhi's fatherhood has three sides. They don't recognize any novelty in the India that attained independence and thereby became a nation. How can it become a nation when it already was—not just already, but always, since ancient times? Such an old nation cannot have a recent father. Then comes the greater status they accord to India as a mother. Yes, there is some scope for discussion on this matter since the territorial geography of India is also *'pitrabhoomi'* or fatherland. However, that does not diminish the value of *'matribhoomi'* or motherland. In the final round, India as mother wins. For that reason, a father figure for the old nation makes no sense. Finally, they repudiated Gandhi as undeserving of any major accreditation. His personality, his tactics, and his failure to snatch the nation intact from foreign hands are all major weaknesses for his eligibility to be called father of the nation.

* * *

Shanties—far messier than those you might see in Mumbai or Delhi—surrounded Bhopal's pesticide plant. To call them slums would be to accord them dignity. They had none. They were hell; the gas leak revealed that hell to all. Like all other Bhopalis of status, all the while I had been busy with Bharat Bhawan's activities, I had never thought about people who lived next to the factory. The terror in their eyes, their choking lungs, their contorted bodies were a surrealistic horror to behold. The slum dwellers were rural migrants. Many had come from far-off regions. Union Carbide punctuated their poverty without giving them a voice, or else their protests over several disasters that had occurred before the big one would have been heard. That's the key feature of industrialization in our conditions: it lends no dignity. Safety was built in the chemical plant, in its manual of procedures, claimed the American engineers who had designed it. They had become indifferent when the company ran into losses in India. Now, it was the Indian partner's responsibility to cut those costs. They did. A local journalist did cry foul, hoping that someone might listen. When the gas started to leak in the night, all was quiet; it only smelt unpleasant.

Pesticide manufacturing in Bhopal brought changes in Madhya Pradesh's landscape within a few years. My home district was among the first to be enrolled into experimental cultivation of high-yielding varieties of wheat. Chemicals that fertilize the soil and kill predators quickly brought the district to global fame. The nation could now aspire for food sufficiency, even surplus. But the chemicals did not stop at the surface of farms; they went into wells and lakes and rivers. And the industry eyed gardens and sold sprays to finish off the miserable burrowers of buds and nibblers of petals. Marigolds, salvias, carnations, roses—they all now looked squeaky clean. No one seemed to notice the absence of earthworms. They used to sprout like short slimy creepers after the inaugural monsoon rain. In autumn and winter, a canopy of butterflies awaited K. and me every Sunday at Gandhi Park where he stood in hard granite at the entrance. Mr Jaiswal, our stern gardening teacher had warned us: catching butterflies is a sin. We committed this sin reluctantly: just once a week.

The chain of decisions and policies binding these changes to Bhopal's midnight hell is neither long nor hard to trace. Was it not nature's revenge? If the instinct for justice can hide under rocks and cause an earthquake, the millions of dead insects have a better case. The scene in Bhopal the next morning offered little room to distinguish humans. They had collapsed in every possible posture, littering the narrow lanes. Running to open spaces proved too hard. Lungs couldn't take the sudden strain. It is said that no accurate count of the dead exists. The disposal of bodies was the first exercise of management that the civil and armed machinery of the state had to perform.

The government's response was to play down the disaster. Perhaps that is not the right term to capture the policy aftermath. Strategies to handle the horror, its memory and its cost had to be worked out. In office parlance, we call it 'fixing the responsibility'. It is an art. Those required to 'fix' are fully aware that their act must not hamper the routine, let alone paralyze it. Escape routes must be woven into the cloth because the State must never feel naked. Bhopal didn't. Its artistic and cultural life kept it going. Inside its social life, the poison proved impervious to aesthetic distraction. Parliamentary elections were to be held later that month. And despite the gas disaster, they were held. A Congress candidate won from Bhopal for the last time.

As a civil servant, you often face a difficult choice—between the truth and the State. You know the truth, but you are called upon to bury it. I don't like putting it like this, and I know many fellow officers would resent it. After Bhopal had burst, we had two immediate tasks on hand: public relief and truth denial. No one said: 'play it down', but every officer spotted it as duty number one. When the State is in trouble, who would stand by it if not the officers? Our political masters have no clue how to handle a disaster, but they know it can be left to us.

Days after the leak, I was transferred—from culture to relief management. My new role was evenly two-pronged: help the victims with State aid, and help the State to bury the truth, starting with numbers. We buried the count of the dead so deep that decades later, no one can say exactly how many died on

day one and then onward. Experts and journalists came from
all over the world, but we didn't let anyone approach accuracy.
They had to accept the wide, vague count, and no one insisted
on separating men from women, adults from children, Hindus
from Muslims. The government was firm about maintaining
ambiguity.

When the internet was born, it caught up with Bhopal.
Hundreds of sites talk about Bhopal; they all politely agree
that between three thousand and sixteen thousand people
were choked to death within days. My job was to document
distress, distribute money and medicines, provide shelter and
food. Those were wretched days. The air must still be toxic, I
often thought. The doubt lingered though no one dared express
it amidst slogan-shouting protestors, media hunters and
lawyers from everywhere. The chief minister was negotiating a
thousand barbs. He took years to confess something that I find
rather touching. In his posthumously published autobiography,
he reveals his secret visit to Allahabad by state helicopter on the
morning of the gas leak. He wanted to pray at the chapel of his
Catholic primary school. It is a heart-rending story, and it must
be true. An affectionate nun must have told the little, lonely
hostel boy to seek God's help when faced with agony.

That winter, the State machinery was struggling with truth
in many cities, including Delhi. Thousands of Sikhs were killed
by riotous mobs enraged by Indira Gandhi's assassination
a month before the Bhopal hell. Estimates of the killed vary
as much as the Bhopal figures. Relief work was as urgent as
the denial of facts. Activists were everywhere, howling for the
truth. Some of them were men and women of reputed integrity.
Negotiation with them was tough, especially on their demand
to catch the culprits—some notorious Congress leaders in
Delhi, and the American chief of Union Carbide in Bhopal
along with his Indian partners.

During those months, I acted like an early inventor of pre-digital fake news. Elsewhere in this book, I have written about all the different shades of meaning Gandhi gave to truth—except one: statistical truth. In Champaran, Gandhi used the power of numbers to prepare his legal case against the British plantation owners. It was a sincere but primitive experiment. In *Hind Swaraj*, he warns against numerical democracy, that is deciding with numbers who should represent and rule. He cautions us against this, but the tone isn't loud. When the election machinery was designed after independence, no one cared to recall Gandhi's warning. He had also mellowed. In any case, *Hind Swaraj* was in disrepute, as an absurd guide for national development. Democracy and development both depend now on statistical management. These days, political parties maintain armies of youthful computer engineers to create booth-wise files for vote garnering.

Truth management is one issue. The other thing about the civil service is that there is no scope for whistleblowing: we are always together. 'Never plead guilty' is the civil servant's code. It applies to everything—including India's favourite word, corruption. If you belong to the top cadre as I did, there is no room for lapses. It is easy to reconcile an officer's *karma* with the Gita's message. You are placed in a situation, under someone who is similarly placed. Your job is pre-defined: follow the rules, comply with decisions taken, implement them. To be part of the bureaucracy means you don't—you can't—question rules and decisions. What does that mean in the middle of a nightmare? When everything melts down, rules can't escape. You lie low, or modestly lie, usually to help the cover-up. When someone is confronting the State with facts, you use your well-thumbed thesaurus and side-track the argument. You stay busy and let truth take care of itself. Reduce its glare. My father must have known this role of a civil servant and still, he wanted me to be one. He was the king's brother and kings are supposed to be above blame. Minions do the needful when kings need truth to be handled. The same occurs in democratic governments. I am sure my father would see no relevance in this para.

In the Bhopal story, there was no room for blowing the whistle at any point—not when the factory was given land so close to the capital city; not when slums grew around the factory; not when its own safety standards fell under cost-cutting measures. Each of these happened at different points in time. The panorama moved across generations of ministers, officers, engineers. On the deadly night, and the morning after, no point was left in reasons. Everyone knew that from now onwards, days, weeks, months, years shall pass in orderly courts, the assembly and the parliament. There was no point worrying, let alone feeling sorry. All must contribute when truth's wildness is at stake. I was no exception, and that's the main point now when I am so worked up about the city's choice of its representative in parliament.

There is no point in becoming a fugitive at this point. Rather, it's time to tell myself that if I compromised with truth, others too have this right. 'Was Gandhi a fugitive?' Had I asked this to my father, his answer would have been quick and categorical: 'Gandhi was a lifelong fugitive. He never ran an office. He wouldn't have known the compulsions of authority and power. His message of courage and bravery in the cause of truth was lofty, saintly—not to last for long.' Why do I have to ask my father when I know that Gandhi's truth has to be re-discovered each time things go out of hand? Why should I care if my father wouldn't like seeing me so tormented? I don't need his authority now. But I can also hear K.'s mother:

'Why do you feel so broken? Be a man.'

'I was, aunty . . .'

'You still are . . . you've done what you could.'

'That didn't help. It doesn't help.'

'I know what you're saying, Munna. Things don't work out the way we wished. Look at me. Partition finished us. But we had to carry on . . . and we did.'

'I know, but you must tell me that there is life after bulldozing.'

'Yes, there is. Didn't you hear K.'s father say, Rome was not built . . .'

'In a day,' I complete her sentence and laugh because I used to ask uncle, 'How long did Rome take to build?' and he too would laugh and say, 'It's only a proverb . . . It means nations can't be built fast; they take their own time.'

'But why must they turn to self-destruction?'

Aunty's voice faded out, and all I could hear was my own answer: 'It happens when the self is not real.' Secular nationalists thought they had done a good, durable job of defining India's self. In the early 1970s, after the spectacular victory over Pakistan, Indira Gandhi inspired many secular-left liberals to believe that the threat of communal dividers was nearly over. They were busy running schools, quietly stitching a different dress for India's self.

Hatred is not a sanctioned feeling; bitterness is. Even if you don't spread hatred, it is not a good emotion. In Christianity, Gandhi found the complete rejection of hate, and he applied it to his adversarial relationship with the British. Bitterness, however, is not untraceable in his writings and speeches, especially the ones he made in his early phase in India. His 1916 address to the jewel-covered sponsors of the Banaras Hindu University shows both anger and bitterness. The Quit India speech also carries traces of bitterness—arising from failed patience. In our times, his tolerance looks loftier than it actually was. Of course, this realization would have made little difference to Savarkar's feelings towards him. Savarkar's followers today are aware of Gandhi's instrumental value. They will use him for their own power game, which they started long ago after getting rid of him.

Hatred is not socially acceptable, but hating does carry some solace. If your castle is now a heap of rubble, and you can only stand by like a stooped-over chikungunya patient contorted by pain, hating helps. Forgiving them would further dilute my redemption. I doubt if Gandhi would approve of this despite his boundless compassion. On his death, Mountbatten compared him to Jesus and the Buddha. In the next round of revision, history books will use Mountbatten's quote as evidence of Gandhi's complicity with the British.

My sense of guilt accompanies me as I descend into recent history. I feel like Dante descending into the different rings of purgatory and hell, with Virgil, the Roman poet, holding his hand. On the heels of unparalleled suffering, Bhopal gifted its vote to the religious separatists. Within a few years of the nightmare, a retired top bureaucrat turned himself into a Hindu leader. He reaped the discontent, while his party translated public resentment into religious separatism. He won Bhopal's parliamentary seat in 1991, and then kept winning it again and again and again. His success branded the Hindu–Muslim cleavage into a fresh code of efficiency, purity, propriety. Its flag bearers mastered the art of turning voters around into permanent delusion and hope. They used Gandhi's words, phrases, thoughts and images, re-writing the copyright in their name, like the re-mix of a Hindi film song. No one dared recall the original. Such intellectual daring would soon become a legal nightmare.

Bharat Bhawan had given Bhopal a splendid aura. The idea, the architecture, the arrival of top artistes, regular programmes—it all lent exuberance to the city. Then came the catastrophe. The images of the immediate aftermath did not last long in the media, and the government put up a big show to claim normalcy. Bharat Bhawan also tried celebrating life in the city of death. *Bargo Basant Hai*—a vernacular adaptation of *A Midsummer Night's Dream* was staged a few months after the gas tragedy. It made little difference. How could it? People were dying a slow death. Opposition to the government came from several sources, but the only thing that improved was the concealment of reality. Politically, the game was over for Bhopal's Congress leadership. Religious fanaticism made deep inroads from both sides of the Hindu–Muslim divide. The new social reality was way beyond the arts to grapple with. Bhopal's all-round descent had begun. Bharat Bhawan was young and somewhat arcane; it had hardly sunk into the public space when the gas tragedy struck Bhopal. The political fallout of the gas finished the dream. The city had already gone over to the lotus party; when Madhya Pradesh shifted to the party in 2004, the capture of Bharat Bhawan proved easy. How naïve, to believe that arts can stem social rot.

Representation is a difficult matter. A member of Parliament represents more than a million people. It is a great idea that one man or woman stands for such a large number. Gandhi had assumed that the Congress was the sole representative of the Indian people and he was the sole representative of the Congress. But it didn't work out at the Round Table conferences. They had every right and reason to ask for the basis of his claim since he was not an elected leader. Even his leadership of the Congress was a matter of belief—in the authenticity of the party's functioning. Under the present electoral system, parties are gigantic lobbies which act like power brokers between vested interests. A party can choose whosoever it wishes to fight an election on the party ticket. The voters need not concern themselves with the candidate's integrity. Once a candidate has won, he serves like a slave of his party in parliament. Gandhi's commentary on the British parliament in *Hind Swaraj* foreshadows today's condition of democracy in India. Bhopal is a minor victim, an example of this national perversity. For the new member of Parliament to represent Bhopal, you don't need to find any real links or affectionate relations.

Bhopal's VIP culture was centred on the civil service class. It formed a hard core that the political class, the MLAs, the ministers and their minions could not soften one bit, let alone penetrate. Democracy meant little to a city where anyone who had a job in an office acted like an officer. The real officers—the ones at the top and those just below them—enjoyed life, in their PWD bungalows and State vehicles. Their wives led a charmed life, supervising servants to keep the dinner table ready to receive the sahib and his friends who might show up without notice. The servants themselves were borrowed from the office. As one might expect, sycophancy hung like a permanent cloud—everywhere. Not that people wanted to please: they thought they had to. You couldn't get people to talk straight—even at a literary gathering. Journalists knew the code so well they never faltered. Many were officially provided decent government quarters. Book launches were frequent. Few officers read little apart from file notes, but there were writers among them—genuine writers and poets too. Bhopal was an aesthetic hub. Its lake, its softly undulating hills, the grassy lawns in front of bungalows, and the cool breeze that laid the night to rest when the guests had left—it was so dreamy you could hardly miss democracy. Wily politicians and their trained secretaries ensured that procedures were never ignored. Alarms had no place. That is why Rajkumar Keswani's 1982 article did not attract big-sized ears. He had warned that the pesticide factory might explode any day. Two years on, it did.

Politicians formed the other big group of the comfortable in Bhopal. They lived on intrigue, just like their political ancestors—the little monarchs of princely states like my own. Before the start of lotus rule, regimes came and departed like seasons, leaving neither mark nor memory behind. Some of the chief ministers lasted for days. The public got used to the idea that democracy was mainly about the tussle between the Brahmans and the Thakurs, and the chief minister is the heart of modern governance.

Individually, many Hindu nationalist men and their wives came across as decent people. Their own minds didn't seem to matter when organizational decisions were involved. Their Swadeshi platform didn't come in the way of any policy changes. Indigenous seeds, organic manures, local products—it all turned out blah blah blah when the government promoted genetically modified seeds that required specific brands of soil enrichers and pest killers. Their duplicity did not embarrass them. That we tried and no one in our own government heard us might have been a decent thing to say. That's not their style; the Swadeshi brigade was one of the many tongues of the party and the government. The lure of an ideological dream—who can doubt that it's coming closer?—overran both collective and individual civility. The closer they come to their goal, the more indifferent they are becoming to the collateral consequences of their unabashed politics.

It's common knowledge that one can't argue with them. That, however, was never my problem. I had been waiting for years to talk to someone from their side about Israel and Pakistan. I'm sure these questions have occurred to others. The questions are hardly unique or sharp-edged. I have nursed them, hoping that a day would come when I could seek an answer. Then, one day, the occasion came—at the palliative intellectual-care centre for the retired where I sometimes go. A senior member of the Development Dialogue Centre organized a meeting. Four of us represented the SN (secular nationalist) side, facing a guest of status in the HN (Hindu nationalist) world. He agreed to have lunch with us. It was a pleasant surprise to have someone of his persuasion for well over two hours. The long wait my questions had endured ended that afternoon. That evening, I went back home with that twisted happiness that truth alone can offer even if it is empty.

'This is something I've wondered about for a long time. Please don't mind my asking why your party admires Hitler?'

Our guest was ready with his reply:

'He was such a great patriot . . . He wanted to make Germany the greatest nation on earth.'

'He killed six million Jews.'

'That is matter of history . . . I mean why it happened.'

I left it at that and went on to ask my real question:

'So, you admire Hitler, but you also admire Israel . . . Isn't that a contradiction?'

'No, no. There is no contradiction . . . Don't you think Israel is a role model of self-confidence . . . It's surrounded by hostile Muslim nations. They got together to attack Israel . . .'

'There would have been no Israel without the holocaust . . .'

'That's a different matter. Hitler was dedicated to his nation . . . He is an icon of patriotism . . . someone ready to go any length for his country.'

I felt a little impatient.

'I find it strange that you don't see a contradiction between your devotion to Hitler and Israel at the same time.'

'Contradiction is only a perception. We take an objective view of things . . . We don't mix them up as some of our academics do.'

The conversation made me realize its futility. Liberals believe in talking across positions, even poles. We don't mind wasting some time; the Hindu-centric rebuilders of India don't. They talk within the fold. They treat it like a family. We might think they are illogical. Well, their logic is their ideology. It gives them a goal, and that's all that matters. Their overarching logic is: all means are equally good if they help to achieve the desired end. The tight fit between means and ends was sacred to Gandhi. He tied a knot between them. Cut it, and you're released from the bonds of morality. You can now frame your foes, publicize lies, destroy institutions, for the sake of election success. It feels great. Your goals come closer towards you. They also *look* right and those who say they are part of an evil design look like worthless people. You are unstoppable, unscrupulous, a visionary.

I remember another clarifying bit from that meeting. It was about the Partition and the creation of Pakistan. Our guest was pleased with himself that he was so candid with us. 'We normally don't face such fundamental questions,' he complimented us— for touching the heart of the matter:

'Hindu nationalists were against the Partition and Pakistan. They still are . . .' I said.

'Of course . . . the Partition was a terrible mistake. Gandhi ji should have resisted it . . . He could have prevented it.'

'Supposing it had been averted . . . An undivided India would have had a greater proportion of Muslims.'

'Yes, I know that, but our country would be intact.'

'Would you tolerate them any better if they were more in number?'

Our pleasant guest spent a few seconds looking around, perhaps tracing a bypass. Then he found it.

'We've never believed in appeasement . . . Numbers don't matter. It's a matter of principle.'

'Yes, I realize that, but I thought you might agree that Partition gave you some relief.'

He could have said, 'How can you talk like that?' But that would be too normal. He said,

'Not at all . . . Our Muslim policy would have been the same as it is now . . . We are not scared of them.'

Not to fear Muslims is fundamental to Hindu nationalism. As an ideology, it stands on an emotive consensus: Hindus are mild and tolerant, Muslims are tough and aggressive. The history of Muslim invasions and conquest teaches that. The lesson means that we Hindus must change, cure ourselves of softness. No more timidity. It must be surgically removed, as shown in Bhisham Sahni's Partition novel *Tamas*. It describes the therapy that the Hindu nationalists of Rawalpindi selected for curing Hindu weakness. While the therapy is trivial, the reading is tough. That's probably why Indira Gandhi chose to serialize the book on State TV. She wanted to expose her challengers. She was expecting too much. Most viewers didn't understand the title *Tamas;* they assumed that it referred to Partition itself, the event, its aftermath. They were not entirely wrong as it was a dark phase of history. A title like '*Andhera*' would have conveyed that, and it would have been more consistent with Bhisham Sahni's lucid style. Why did he choose a Sanskrit expression? He must have looked for an antonym of truth and found it in '*tamas*'. It signified darkness of the mind unlit by truth or its need.

Be that as it may, Hindu nationalism is a historical force. We, the secular nationalists, have not granted it legitimacy—as a product of colonialism. The West serves Hindu nationalists as the ideal to be achieved, in military might and material prosperity. Flyovers, highways, bullet trains, weapons-manufacturing— these are their favourite symbols of progress. They internalized them, along with orientalism that drives them to define India in terms of its ancient myths. It serves as a wonderful veneer for their copying instinct. Gandhi does not attract them, but his popularity troubles them. It also puzzles them. He played all the wrong tunes they think and yet managed to draw people.

They attribute his success to a mixture of seductive appearance and cunning. Many of his ideas and aims repel them, especially his goal of bonding Hindus and Muslims. That is one thing they can't tolerate. Their minds are stuck in the history of Muslim rule.

These irritants—and many more—are nicely covered in Godse's final statement in court. I believe he was allowed to read it out in full because it had merit in the eyes of so many. How many assassins get this kind of sponsored opportunity? Even if there is controversy over the original author of the speech Godse delivered, the statement matters. He read it aloud, and with passion enough to make the crowd—both men and women—audibly sob. They saw truth in it; not Gandhi's truth, of course. We may wish to think that the sobbing court crowd was responding to the milieu—the awful riots, Gandhi's pro-Muslim stance, and so on. But the error of this view has been proved by Godse's persistent presence. It is comforting to call it a fringe presence. Secular nationalism is fond of many such comforts.

No one remembers the assassins of Lincoln, Kennedy or Martin Luther King. Godse's case is unique. His fame never stopped growing. Hindi satirist Harishankar Parsai made a prediction. A time will come, he wrote in the 1970s, when Gandhi will be known as the man Godse had killed.

We aren't quite there yet but moving along. Let me translate Rajesh Joshi's 2019 poem: 'the tidal waves raised by a fistful of salt have retreated/dead fish, snails and crabs litter the sand.' Joshi lives in Bhopal: I can imagine how distraught Joshi feels. Wilful distortion of history and the use of schools for injecting young minds with lies are pushing us towards the day when Parsai's prognosis will come true. A general knowledge test for boys and girls taken recently gave these four choices in a question asking how Gandhi died: old age, illness, murder, suicide. The fourth choice was to be adjudged the right answer. No one was alarmed when a Hindi daily published this as news.

* * *

Khairun was the only Muslim girl in my class in the 'basic' primary school at Kundeshwar. That morning K.'s class teacher was on leave, so his class was told to join ours. He sat down next to me. Khairun was sitting behind us. She was a more competent spinner than either of us. But that day she was having trouble keeping her right hand steady. Each time she stretched her hand, the thread broke, and she muttered something. When it happened a third time, I turned my head around and said something nasty. She ignored me, but K. heard my words, and he repeated them. Khairun was a stout little girl who took no nonsense from anyone, but our joint verbal assault and the recalcitrant thread proved too much that day. She answered us, but all we could hear was a sob. Our teacher also heard it. When he asked us to stand up, we thought we were going to face trouble. He took us out of the craft room and asked:

'Do you know what you were doing?'

We stood silent and he carried on.

'You have no idea what you were doing. Teasing anyone is bad but teasing Khairun? That's very bad . . . And I will tell you why . . .'

By now, he was visibly angry. We had never seen him like that. We knew we were in for something. What we got, though, was not a dressing down: it just felt like that. It was the first political lesson of our lives.

Our teacher told us that it is *our* responsibility to make Khairun happy *because she is a Muslim.* Her uncle could have easily sent her to Pakistan, but he didn't because he trusted India. Many Muslims had gone, and Khairun's parents had also decided to go. They lived in Bhopal. They took a train to Bombay, and from there they would have gone to Karachi by boat, but the train was blown up before it reached Bombay. Khairun survived but she lost both her parents. 'Her uncle brought her here and that is why she studies with you,' our teacher said, bringing the story to a close, looking at us as if we were guilty of doing the terrible things he had narrated. Then, after a brief pause, he said: 'You should never forget what Gandhi ji has told us—that if you behave like a good Hindu, then every Muslim will respect you.'

I am not sure if I understood the lesson right, but something must have sunk in. Or else, perhaps, the image of a Muslim being lynched wouldn't trouble me these days. 'I am sorry I failed you,' I tell my teacher and Khairun. I don't know how things got this far; a lifetime has slipped away, and the world has changed. The fact is I forgot Khairun. Childhood memories go into a coma; they return when things go wrong— so wrong that you can't make sense of anything anymore. It's like a dramatic return to babyhood. It's hard to wake up when you're rolling down a gentle slope at a comfortable speed. That's how India was, Bhopal was, before Gujarat happened. I should have remembered Khairun when the news of those riots was coming in. She too probably thought of two small boys and the teacher who had told them to look after her. How awful it all feels now when it is so late. You can hardly intervene in a lynching. You worry about yourself. You find a hundred good reasons to stay away, to watch and do nothing. We are all burnt out now, and Khairun might have gone too. She and I and K. were all little spinners. We were taught how to tie tiny knots when the thread broke, but we stopped spinning when our childhoods ended. We were members of Gandhi's fancy, great dream. When the dream ended, we were asleep and didn't notice.

A few years ago, K. showed me a study of small children in old Delhi. The researcher found that children as young as four and five had negative views about the 'other' religious group. A sharp finding of this study was that Hindu children had more negative stereotypes of Muslims than Muslim children of the same age as Hindus. A few years later, I met a nine-year-old village girl from eastern UP who had been warned by her mother about Muslims. They are so bad, she told me, that they can harm you if they just look at you from a distance. With ideas like that so firmly established in a young mind, we can hardly claim any right to be surprised by what has happened in the plains of UP in recent years.

Munna died as the lockdown started. Had he lived for a little longer, he might have found some solace in an unusual media story. It showed that the lotus party had not completed its mission, even in Uttar Pradesh under a holy-looking leader. While countless numbers of migrant labourers were fleeing the metro cities on foot, Amit and Yakoob were lucky to find a truck to ferry them from Surat to Lucknow. When the truck was crossing Shivpuri, Amit became feverish. Others who were stuffed in the truck got panicky that they would catch the virus, so they asked the driver to drop Amit—on the highway. It was high noon in the third week of May. The driver stopped the truck and asked Amit to get down. His Muslim friend could not bear to carry on. He later told a journalist: 'Our parents in the village were waiting . . . What would

I say to his parents?' He also got off.
Sitting on the highway, he held Amit's head
in his lap, sprinkling what water he had.
By the time help arrived to take the two to
a hospital, Amit had died. Yakoob was put
in an isolation ward. The rampant campaign
against Muslims impelled someone to ask:
'Would a Muslim in Pakistan care like this
for a Hindu living there?'

We who wear the secular chip on our shoulder labelled Godse
a 'Hindu fanatic'. We ignored his inspiration and training.
Godse was part of the Hindu nationalist *parivar*—something
the judiciary didn't recognize at the time. An extended family
is more than a network in the modern sense, but less than a
family, allowing members to disperse, come close, stay in touch,
depending on circumstances. Godse was like that—an inspired
member of the *parivar*. People who praise him these days
are inspired too. They have an inner urge to set things right.
Nurturing this urge is part of a programme—for boys. Sunset
drills and lessons in the power of unity sustain their zeal to
pursue the goal of corrective action. They are soldiers of India's
destiny that awaits the right moment of history. An endemic
dispute continues to rage in their minds between Godse and
Gandhi. No one who has not been part of the daily sunset
training can describe the dispute. If you assume it is complex,
you are wrong. Any nuanced description—of the kind secular
historians love giving—will fail to explain the passion Godse
and his associates need to get rid of Gandhi. Killing is difficult
to manage without strong enough passion. Usually, the desire
to kill needs to be sustained for a while until the moment for
action is reached. You need plenty of dislike to maintain the
killing impulse; in fact, you need a considerable build-up of

hatred. How long was that period for Godse? The wide terrain of his complaints suggests that Gandhi must have stung him for years.

Let me work out Godse's greatest charge. It was about manhood, the opposite of everything feminine. Like his kindred souls, Godse wanted India to be manly—meaning strong, fearless and aggressive. A man, they believe, is someone who does not hesitate to punch his foe in the face. Eyes, jaw, teeth, all are fair targets. Godse was irked by Gandhi's continuous harping on non-violence. Hindus have suffered so much from non-violence, and this old man wants more of it. We lost out to Muslims *because* we were non-violent. We can't afford it anymore. We can't allow this strange fellow to emasculate us any further. This charge of Godse goes in every direction. Who could challenge him in the court that his argument about language was absurd? He found Gandhi's advocacy of Hindustani one more emasculating strategy. It involved letting Urdu words mix into Hindi. That's what would make it Gandhi's Hindustani. Urdu words are not words—they are Muslim.

As an emotion, hatred tends to grow incrementally, feeding on itself. It also feeds on jealousy, and Godse's speech does indicate he was jealous of Gandhi, his popularity and his ardent following. Godse's verbal attack on Gandhi must have attracted a lot of people. A judge who was part of the bench hearing the Gandhi murder case has said that if the people sitting in the courtroom when Godse was speaking—and the room was packed—were asked to give *their* verdict as a public jury, they would have exonerated Godse. Other accounts of that period resonate similar feelings in the public ethos of Delhi and Punjab. Through his act and public self-defence, Godse expressed the emotions suffused in the post-Partition ethos of northern India. It is possible that many people had felt like him but could not sustain hatred for as long as Godse had. It explains the fascination he evoked. The news of the shooting aroused public emotion of a kind never seen before, bringing the riots to an instant halt. By the time Godse's trial concluded, the tide of penitence had ebbed. In the years that followed Godse's hanging, the political milieu came under new pulls and pressures. Nehru's towering presence shaped the nascent phase of India's encounter with freedom. The grudge with Gandhi also grew. Hindu nationalists never abandoned their cause or lost a moment's hard work.

Friends who live in Bhopal have taken the election in their stride saying that any other city would have returned Bhopal's candidate with a reasonable majority. They also say that the Godse aspect was hardly important for anyone. The lotus was. The party's nominee for the Bhopal seat showed it could now afford to be audacious—in whichever context it chooses to show off its manly invincibility. How could I feel so hurt, one of my friends asked. Wasn't it inevitable? Yes, of course, he expected me to say. When you're sick at heart, you lose enough of your memory to feel struck by something new.

It was the annual function of a reputed elite school. Amidst a number of songs and dances, the turn came of an ensemble based on Gandhi's famous composition, 'Raghupati raghav raja ram.' The music and the singing—in which hundreds of children of different ages were participating—were truly beautiful and uplifting. For a moment, one felt emotionally transported. Then, as the song proceeded, I realized something strange. The original composition has just four lines. The third line, I realized, was missed even as the second and the fourth or last line kept getting repeated. The missing third line was 'Ishwar Allah tero naam': 'Ishwar' and 'Allah' (both) your names. This was not sung; it was edited out. Someone in that great school did not like the idea that 'Allah' should be treated as just another name of God. When the song was over, another performance started and the lovely afternoon changed. This was one of the thousands of moments pushing me to tell myself: India is changing. How could I not be prepared for worse things to happen on a bigger, terrifying scale?

Gandhi changed India. More accurately, he moulded the changes India was going through during the decades that followed his return from South Africa. There, the fight for justice with legal instruments slowly turned into a political struggle. The South Africans couldn't make sense of this mutation. Leaving the struggle incomplete, so to say, Gandhi returned to India's battlefield—uncharted, diffuse, heaving like a ship without a navigating device. Gandhi's initial rounds in India too were legal, but then a sociology unknown to the living generation took over. His vague description of this sociology that he had set out in *Hind Swaraj* was not easy to decipher. (It still isn't.) It contained a critique of society and culture, leading to an opening in ideas and values long disused and lost. Within a few years, his comrades could feel something new in their hands. It was a code, politically encrypted, but essentially moral. It was a new version of some old ideas drawn from different philosophical sources, but also from traditions that were still alive in villages and small towns. Over time, they became the defining markers of Gandhi's political hold.

They hardly looked like the kind of weapons that might help India fight European domination. They still don't, and they are very different from the tools the Hindu-centric politicians are using these days to show off their and India's arrival in the comity of powerful nations. Ideas like truth and non-violence, indifference to material might and prosperity were unfamiliar, even amusing, for India's British rulers and other European powers. They took time to recognize the freak strategies Gandhi was repeatedly using, each time with some more success in the social sphere. He knew what he was doing, and the distance he would have to cover. He became a symbol of slow running.

Once you're touched by fear, it's hard to shake it off. I have felt it many times since I started writing this book, so I know. What am I afraid of, I ask, hoping that the question would release me, that it would at least remind me of where I am in my life, well past career anxieties. This short meditation helps, but only for a short while. I know how many retired civil servants like me feel uncomfortable in India's changed climate. Some feel mortified. Quite a few have lost the hope that things would improve within their remaining lifetime. Because of this bleak prognosis, they choose to stay silent. A short while ago, more than a hundred of them wrote an open letter, expressing anxiety, suggestive of outrage, over the damage being done to key institutions such as the judiciary and the Election Commission. Nothing much happened, but the return of silence was ominous. E-protests about lynching, bulldozing, fake encounters, raids, and so on made no impact. Perhaps something was quietly conveyed to these armchair protestors. Phrases like 'urban naxals' were invented to brand intellectuals and academics as enemies of the nation. Journalists and editors experience this kind of silent communication, advising them to keep their mouths shut, their lips pursed. So, when fear placed its hand on my shoulder, I was ready for it. If fear stalks the land, how could I be spared? I am still writing because I have not forgotten that I have to express myself freely. It now depends on what you want to express.

Like a folk physician, Gandhi diagnosed this as our number one ailment. Colonial rule couldn't be fought, he thought, so long as people were scared of it. And not just colonial rule; advocates of violent resistance also nourish fear. Speaking against them also needed courage. Gandhi's therapy against fear made the pursuit of truth possible. Fear is now back. Secular writers say that Muslims are now scared; of course, they are, but it's not Muslims alone. Anyone who wants to scream is scared: to say *that* is also culpable. Oppressors turn up all over social media, ready to troll you. I have tried to sustain my nerves and spirit to carry on with this book. It blows a lot of whistles. It feels silly to do so. Isn't a whistle blown best when you blow it once? As a government servant, I knew you couldn't go far in rank unless you tolerate the State's lies. Whistle-blowing has no career dividend to offer, even in retirement, though it is tempting to set records straight. Bhopal's record is so crooked, that no amount of delayed whistleblowing can help. My whistle is damp, blown long after the lies were told.

I am fortunate that my life coincided with a period of history when Gandhi's imprint had not completely faded out, nor had anyone tried to wipe it off. In fact, no one was trying to compete with Gandhi. The country deviated from a lot of things he symbolized, and the general mood was that we could not meet Gandhi's standards. It was a humble submission, so to say. We are now in a new phase when every attempt is being made to consign Gandhi to the dustbin of history. A way of thinking that his moral power should not gain traction has come into dominance by hook and by crook. No one feels certain that history will turn back, proving Gandhi to be immortal. For me, it's time to express personal gratitude.

Now that we are set to lose what we had gained under Gandhi's leadership, it is good to remember how difficult the task was he had given himself. Nor is it a bad idea to acknowledge his partial success. He is now a frozen symbol, a statue in granite or cast metal, standing on modest pedestals in many parks and at the gate of buildings where people perform weighty tasks. In the darkness of a moonless night, the rocky figure comes alive at times when a lapwing crosses the sky, shrieking '*you did it, you did it!*' In his authoritative volume on Indian birds, Salim Ali mentions an alternative script to translate the intrepid lapwing's

shriek: '*pity to do it, pity to do it!*' Salim Ali's alternative version
resonates with the state of my mind after spending these past
few months with Gandhi. India's rejection of Gandhi is a loss
for every nation, for India alone could afford to live some of
Gandhi's precepts and critiques. He wanted us to be different
and original. He warned us against conforming—to the mighty,
who are proud of their bombs; the glitterati who steal. Copying
would ruin us and extinguish the hope that we might have
shown the emergency escape.

For gratitude, Sanskrit has a pithy term, not difficult to
translate, but hard to melt into life and meaning. 'Kritagya'
breaks up into 'krita': work long finished. Staying aware of it is
'gya'. The knowledge that someone did it for us is not the same
thing as keeping that memory alive in everyday awareness. It is
not like naming a good guy at the end of the news and playing
the ditty he was fond of. Nor is gratitude what you offer to the
good doctor after he has saved you. Mine is like that. It is a bit
embarrassing that I treated Gandhi like medicine. If I were a
bit younger, I might have faced my country's dark night with
plans for impossible missions.

Gandhi was like that. 'A votary of truth,' he wrote, is
'often obliged to grope in the dark'. Many groping moments
of his life are diligently recorded in his autobiography as if to
highlight his courage to be an eccentric, an extremist, an urban
naxal. The episodes create suspense as much as irritation, and
the reading is lucid, not necessarily pleasant. Bizarre, you say,
even as you're astonished by the child-like transparency of the
text and the man. On sex, his views and conduct are steeped
in old beliefs that are now rarely articulated though they have
not disappeared. On sickness and medicine, his derision of
doctors is shocking enough, but some of the stories of self-
cure, suffering and nursing verge on horror. One shows how he
walked with a straight back though he was nervously groping.

His ten-year-old son was once close to death and Gandhi was bent on treating him with his own awkward methods, ignoring the doctor. What kind of man was he, you ask, and the answer is categorical: there is no one of his kind we are going to see— someone who didn't give two hoots for normalcy. Einstein was right in his forecast that future generations would refuse to believe that such a man existed at all. They routinely do so these days, on WhatsApp and other platforms, with videos to convey deeper credibility than does the autobiography.

Gandhi's killer(s) thought he would do more damage if he lived any longer even though he was old and tottering. He had irked them long enough, and now, after Partition, he was demanding justice for Muslims and Pakistan. Apparently, Gandhi saw truth in upholding Muslim interests on both sides of the border. His truth was not mere minority protection. Rather, it was the best moment for Hinduism to forgive the excesses of past Muslim rulers. In the months before Partition, Gandhi unabashedly showed his pain over the suffering of Muslims, just as much as he partook of the pain of Hindu refugees pouring into the Indian Punjab and Delhi. Evening after evening, he spoke of his agony and prayed, and did not agree to receive police protection.

Those who disliked him did so because they could not imagine how—and why—a Hindu should worry about Muslims? Gandhi stretched his comprehensibility all his life, but especially towards its end. Not just his adversaries, his close colleagues and friends also found it hard to make sense of his ideas and moves. He was difficult to deal with although he was always pleasant and sometimes child-like. British officers were never sure what to expect during his unending campaigns. Everyone who knew him was familiar with his penchant to argue out an impossible position. He took all tough turns and bends as tests of willpower: if only he could sustain his will to see something happen, it would. And it did, a number of times. Seeking his own end through a violent assault was also an act of will, and he made it happen. We who must deal with Gandhi in retrospect have no choice in calling it an act of martyrdom. For him, it was the only reasonable end.

What he achieved by choosing to die through murder is easy to assess. To Hindu society, I think, he presented an unfamiliar emotion through the mode of his death. If there is one emotion that Hinduism, in its epic narratives, does not exemplify, it is any sense of collective guilt. Hindu society would be radically different for women if a sense of guilt were part of the inheritance of the two great epics, the Mahabharata and the Ramayana. In the presence of her husbands and other close relatives, Draupadi faced public humiliation, that too in her own palace. Every Indian boy and girl encounter this episode with shock and disbelief when they hear it first. How could this happen, they ask their elders, hoping that they probably know more. But they don't; so, all they can say is: yes, it was very bad. That's all. Three millennia have passed, and no one, certainly no man, feels a pang of guilt. As a male child, you learn to view the story as something horrible happening to a helpless woman. You conclude that such things happen to women. No man needs to feel responsible for what Draupadi suffered. Some even justify it with tortuous explanations.

The same can be said of Sita, the modest heroine of the Ramayana. The so-called test—*agni pareeksha*—that she had to go through after Rama's victory and her release from Ravana's captivity is a story that ought to make us all feel the pangs of guilt, but such pangs are not a part of our cultural inheritance. Gandhi's assassination shook millions when they heard about it. Those who witnessed the aftermath say that people felt as if they had made an awful mistake.

All India Radio's live coverage of Gandhi's funeral carries plenty of evidence of the unbearable shame and collective regret. Grown-up men and women were crying like children. The sense of loss was personal, say many eyewitness accounts. But the wailing crowds couldn't have known that, during the few seconds left of his life, Gandhi was kind to his killer, concerned about *his* safety. It was no extraordinary conduct for him. All his life, he had aspired to live without fear. He had also aspired, for a long time, to meet his Maker as unblemished as possible. Concern for adversaries had shaped his politics, keeping it open, shunning conspiratorial instincts. The pistol in Godse's hand told Gandhi that the moment he had been waiting for had arrived. As the news of the assassination spread, waves of turmoil spread across the nation. It caused a scare, then relief—that the killer was not a Muslim. Millions felt an unfamiliar feeling—a sense of guilt for the mode of Gandhi's death. The effect was dramatic. Uncanny peace descended on riot-torn cities. Hatred towards Muslims abated.

The Hindu nationalist ideology has no room for guilt or remorse of any kind: pride is all it fertilizes. The narrative of victimhood justifies everything—especially Muslim muzzling. 'Say with pride we're Hindu', was one of the slogans used during the early days of political mobilization. That phase is a distant memory now. The co-option of Hindu traditions, symbols and ideals has reached an advanced stage. Gandhi has also been co-opted; his symbolic value accommodated in a new pantheon. Tall metallic statues surround his meek figure. Engineers and managers utilize Gandhian relics at will, to give events and places an authentic look. It's time I said to Gandhi: bye and thanks. I want to say, abide with me, but I don't know where I might take him along for comfort.

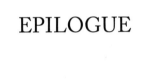

EPILOGUE

The task Munna had given me is over at last. It was tough and not always pleasant, but I am glad I have finished it and I now feel relieved. I was not afraid of the strain it would imply, or the pain it might bring, of remembering him in his last days. Right from the start, I had assumed that working on Munna's 'G' files would gratify me and mitigate my grief over the loss of an old and dear friend. But as soon as things got underway, I recalled the conflicts I would have to negotiate to derive any pleasure from what he had left for me to do or even the satisfaction of doing it. I knew from the experience of my own writing in recent years that I did not have much stamina for dealing with dilemmas about what to include and exclude so that the text doesn't end up in controversy.

My idea of making it a joint project didn't get me far. All I could do was insert my thoughts or news about things that had happened after Munna's death. My italicized additions gave certain portions the feel of a dialogue between us. It is his book, I had to remind myself in order to keep my inserts short. Had he not died in the first wave of Covid, my role would have probably been merely to react to certain portions or points during conversations. That would have left him free to re-write if he wanted to. How much easier that would have been! Here I was, left alone to make sense of what he had wanted to convey, and then to edit it.

Despite my best efforts to resist, gloomy thoughts, again and again, clouded my mind and my energy to work on Munna's text. He was a doer, not much interested in writing. 'If we can do something, isn't it better than writing about it?' he sometimes said on phone, reacting to my commentary published in that day's paper. I never agreed with that view of writing as I believe writing has its own pleasure and purpose even if it is about hopeless situations. Munna's manuscript was about a supremely unpleasant subject: the loss of Gandhi's many gifts to us as a nation. I doubt if writing on this subject gave him any real pleasure, except for a moment now and then when he might have gloated over a sharp phrase or choice of word. But it gave him something to stay engaged with during the last and very difficult phase of his life. This is not a convenient thing to say, I suppose, about someone who took Gandhi so seriously and used his absence to re-examine everything, including his own life. It gave him an anchor to hold on to when he was losing his grip on his world as he had known it.

The files he had sent to me a few days before he passed away were difficult to make sense of. Not a single file was complete, and some were difficult to place in any clear connection with the rest. It was obvious that Munna was using writing in order to heal and explore himself, treating Gandhi as a resource to soothe his wounded sensibility and conscience. He seemed to have inspired himself by complaining to Gandhi. The fantasy that Gandhi was listening and talking to him apparently gave Munna the vital strength he needed to recover from his shock. His reveries and hallucinations sustained him intellectually through the last months of his life. I could hardly retain all such patches of his text, but I did let a few remain. The portions about contemporary events into which he had dragged Gandhi as a moral compass had to be pruned as well, though for a different reason that the reader will be able to guess.

My pleasure in working on Munna's files diminished as I progressed. The main reason was that I felt compelled to delete more often than I wanted to. Editing does involve deleting, but in this case, deletion became necessary far more often than I could consider reasonable, and there was no question of seeking the author's consent. Nor was there, any point in seeking Pushpa's permission. Here and there I tried to modify Munna's text in order to save it, but this also proved a difficult option because his style was hard to emulate. We could use the musical term *portamento* to describe it: each statement starts smoothly but ends in a clear, almost abrupt pause before the next smoothly expressed idea begins. That's the way Munna used to talk. I can hear his voice, my eyes watching his lips, his small chin, my attention and curiosity waiting to see how he would wrap up an incisive point. In fact, I heard his voice throughout the text of his files, at times from so close up that I felt muddled in my resolve to stay objective like a good editor.

Between feeling sentimental and excited, tired and vague, I struggled with the journey through the ten files. At times, I missed him sorely enough to entertain the thought of abandoning the project altogether, nearly whispering that *no one* knows about it, so it wouldn't matter. At other times, I saw great value in his text and wondered how he had maintained his urge, for as long as he did, to write about a country he found altered beyond recognition or hope of recovery. My reluctance to change his sentences persisted in the same measure as my urge to convey his anxiety about India, and its future. I know from experience that all writing carries this dilemma, but this was different.

Munna's commentary on Truth, posed quite a challenge to edit whereas his reminiscence and discussion of Bhopal

proved the easiest. This may be because I did Bhopal last, and
by that time, I had become quite used to Munna's style. More
likely, Bhopal proved easy because I first had to translate it
from the Hindi original wherein the style was just the same.
While translating Munna's two long files on Bhopal, before
compressing their texts into one, I felt convinced that this
was where this writing project had originated in his mind. At
that point, he probably saw no clear shape in his project, and
most probably, the idea of gratitude to Gandhi came later. The
Bhopal story was too densely packed with personal confessions
to be anything but a moral struggle to redeem one's integrity. I
think it was while going through that struggle that Munna felt
rescued by Gandhi. As evidence of my guess, I offer this extract
from one of the files that I could not accommodate anywhere:

'There are moments in life when you say to yourself: "Yes,
I trust my senses and reasoning—and that's why I see no hope;
not even temporary relief. If reason offers no escape, why
can't I try faith and prayer?" Fine, but can I pray to Gandhi?
When I tried, he forbade me to pray to *him*. "Pray to God,"
he said. Only His feet are worth touching, he told stooped-
over Indians. He comes across as God's intermediary in some
popular episodes of his story. He would have dismissed the
notion outright. How could he have agreed to be seen as God's
intermediary? He depended on God all the time, and not just to
seek inspiration. No, Gandhi went on public record frequently
that he asked God to give him specific guidance, show him
direction. Such a man would hardly appreciate my prayer. All I
can offer him is my gratitude—for giving me a thread to hang
on to. It makes me feel continuous. My best pictures hang on
it, like little festoons. I'm still around, but I know these are not
my times. I am sure I'm not the only one who feels like this.
In the name of the nation we did what we thought best. Many
things we did weren't right or good enough. Who else can hear

my confession but the nation's father? If we feel we are losing
the nation, he must know.'

The thread was always there, but Munna probably caught
it *after* going over his statement of shared guilt. He identified
with the city and its unbearable luck. Then, as he thought it
through, he held himself, at least partly, responsible for the
city's descent. He quoted a Bhopal poet, Dushyant Kumar: 'Is
sire se us sire tak sab sharikey zurm hain/Aadmi ya to zamanat
par riha hai ya farar [From this end to that, all are guilty; one is
either on bail, or absconding].' It made me sad that Munna was
so disappointed with Bhopal's arts' complex, Bharat Bhawan.
He had worked hard to make it a success story. Had he given
me the chance, I would have reminded him how much he
had enjoyed some of the events organized at Bharat Bhawan,
especially plays.

When he was happy, his laughter became an event by
itself. Over dinner after a comic play, he would break off in
the middle of a laugh, as if to say something, then laugh a
little more and louder. We saw *Andher Nagri* together. Bharat
Bhawan had invited Vijay Chauhan to direct it. He had
migrated to Los Angeles, but Munna came to know that he
was on an extended visit to Jabalpur, so he invited Chauhan to
Bhopal and used the Bharat Bhawan repertory to stage a play
of his choice. Vijay Chauhan chose *Andher Nagri*, literally, the
city where nothing is right. It is a nineteenth-century script
by Bharatendu who uses a traditional folk play to mount a
funny allegorical attack on the British raj by portraying a town
where wrong prevails over right. If you are trying to present
social disorder, you cannot better *Andher Nagri*. That evening
Munna was gleeful—over the grand success of a work of art
in highlighting the absurdity of governance, the courts, police
procedures, the malleable witnesses and everything else. I can
still hear Munna's unending laughter that evening. He was

pleased that Bharat Bhawan could stage that play during Indira
Gandhi's Emergency. Was it not seditious? Of course, it was,
and that was Bharat Bhawan's triumph. Why then did Munna
not give Bharat Bhawan, and himself, more credit? His despair
did not permit him to give himself a fair verdict.

I felt uncomfortable that his frequent lapse into a bleak
trance in his writing led him to self-recrimination. Of course,
I knew that in these patches he was worrying about himself.
Engaging with Gandhi so intimately meant that he would view
his career as being that of a cog in the State's wheel, oiling
it, contributing to its kinetic force. Encounters with himself
led, in quite a few such episodes to admitting that he was an
accomplice and, therefore, had no right to indict the saffron
nationalists for changing the nation's climate and direction.
Munna was being unfair to himself in such portions, I felt. Had
he written his autobiography, as many retired civil servants do,
he could have enumerated just as many achievements as any
honest IAS officer.

Alternatively, if his book had not brought Gandhi into so
close a focus, Munna would have presented a fine example of
the struggle many civil servants accept, as their moral duty, to
endure the pressure of power-hungry politicians in order to
make ordinary people's lives a shade better. He had a clean,
bright record, but his delusory brooding that started after
the shock of Bhopal's election stained his image of himself. I
compelled myself to reduce the number of stretches where my
friend had dropped himself into dark reveries, some of which
gave the impression of a spiritual quest. Some I left, with
minor modifications, as instances of his agony and search for
redemption with Gandhi's assistance. To illustrate his gratitude
to the Mahatma, these would suffice, I felt.

Soon after I had acquainted myself with the 'G' files, I
went to his house. Sitting in his study, I looked around at the

considerable collection of books he had assembled on Gandhi. A shiver passed through me as I sat at his desk, and I could hardly focus on the titles on his shelf. Some of the books he had consulted more frequently were lying on the desk. A variety of bookmarks were stuffed into Gandhi's autobiography. I picked up that book and scanned the pages Munna had folded at the top corner. Others had pieces of paper with scribbling, flaps taken off envelopes and objects like toothpicks marking something valuable.

There were notes on the margins of several pages. I tried to read them, tentatively hoping that they might offer some insight into Munna's files. Soon I was overwhelmed and nervous. This is not the way I would ever get on with or complete the posthumous duty he had assigned me, I sternly told myself. I realized I had no choice: I must make whatever sense I could of the text his disparate files carried, go through them all one by one, then turn out a coherent manuscript. A meticulous search for clues to Munna's intent would be of no use. Nor would a bibliography or list of references be worth putting together. In the age of the internet, any good reader desirous of following the names and references could easily do so.

Before finishing my work on this manuscript, I decided to visit Kundeshwar where our friendship had begun. The road to Kundeshwar didn't seem right: it was much too wide. Then, I realized that the double ranks of trees lining it on both sides had all gone. I asked the taxi driver what had happened and when. 'The road had to be widened,' he said. 'Big trucks found it difficult, so they chopped down the trees to widen the road on both sides.' After a pause, he said, 'Now it's concrete, so it'll last.' After another, longer pause, he said, 'They were nice trees. . . mahua, mango, teak, neem and many others.' 'When did it happen?' I asked. He replied, 'Quite recently . . . during Corona.' The conversation didn't end there. 'Some people tried to stop the choppers,' he said. 'They went to court and got a stay, but it was too late . . . The contractor had already sold the wood.' Our Maruti Dzire was moving along on the smooth surface. A tempo was approaching. After it had passed, the driver said, pensively: 'The contractor made a lot of money . . . Development is like that,' he said. We were crossing Ganeshganj. I could see the little village pond from the car window. The modest temple had grown taller. It was freshly painted in white, with impressive rings of saffron brown. They were shining in the October forenoon sun. Beside the temple stood the clay horse, its orange paint changed to yellow.

During one of our car rides to school, Munna had told me the story of this horse. He had heard it from his father. The horse was once real, went the story. A British engineer visited the king, asking for permission to survey the land for a railway line. The king said to the engineer: 'I will give you the permission if your train can run faster than my horse.' On the day of the contest, the horse was taken to a railway station in the adjoining district which was under British rule. The steam engine blew its whistle and the horse started galloping. He was well ahead of the engine for quite some distance. When the engine went past him, the horse galloped even more furiously. Hundreds of people were watching. They cheered him on. They knew he would win, but moments later he collapsed, rolled over and died. His body was brought to Ganeshganj. It is buried beside the temple where the clay horse stands.

A long line of small shops selling trinkets and sweets appeared by the roadside and I didn't even realize that the taxi had reached Kundeshwar. Was my school tucked behind this line? No, where our humble primary school with its spinning wheels and looms and shelves for our clumsy clay toys once stood, there was a flashy, big building, its name painted in large capital letters: SHIV GLOBAL ACADEMY. I told the driver to take me directly to the temple. I took off my shoes to climb the seventeen steps. They were now paved with cream marble. The ancient open temple itself was now surrounded by red-painted walls with ornamental windows and doors that led to smaller temples for different deities. The three brass bells that Munna and I used to stroke with our hands before swinging the clapper, had been replaced by a series of giant-size bells.

I went down the stairs on the other side of the temple. The deep pond looked unchanged, and the river too. Its water was flowing quietly over the cross bridge above the spillway. Just like in the old days, patches of slippery green moss covered the flat surface of the bridge. Walking over it, you had to balance your step against your eyes surveying the irregular stretches of moss to locate the gaps between them. A single step taken haphazardly could be fatal during the rainy months when the current was strong and so noisy that you couldn't hear your friend's warning. Today, the current was gentle, inviting me to try my elderly steps, letting my bare feet feel the cool, clear water, without Munna holding my nervous right hand. I missed him sorely, my eyes blurred in memories, as three boys splashed around in the water below.

I sat down on the steps of the river. A gentle breeze passed through the trees on the other side. Not everything had changed, but Munna had been pushed over, by the tectonic shift in India and his dear Bhopal. It was good that Gandhi had reached out to him, restoring his strength to express his anger and his anguish. He didn't expect to see his dear country rebound. Of course, it can't be the same as it was before the latest in its long history of upheavals. Munna could not wait to see how it would feel when this particular convulsion passed as pass it must. That is Shiva's law. With my feet dabbling in the flowing water, I longed for Munna to hear me say, India is a great teacher, my friend, and it never fails to teach whoever tries to bend it.

The deep pond is there just below the mossy surface of the cross bridge, waiting for the river to renew its onward journey. People used to say a crocodile couple lives in the pond. They are the custodians of the river. That is why it has the name *Jamdhar*, the current of Yama, the God of Death. It falls into the deep pond, then revives itself and flows onward.

Acknowledgements

I express my gratitude to Nidhi Gaur, Ramachandra Guha, Latika Gupta, Phool Chandra Jain, Frances Kumar, Prabhjyot Kaur Kulkarni, the late Gayatri Parmar, Yemuna Sunny and Ashok Vajpeyi.

Scan QR code to access the
Penguin Random House India website